D0115881

Advance Praise for
The Occurrence

"In *The Occurrence*, Desiderio delivers a haunting political thriller that stayed with me long after I turned the last page."

—LeVar Burton

"An intelligent and captivating thriller. *The Occurrence* takes a true-to-life terrorist plot and then twists the story, forcing a reexamination of the reader's faith. I dare you to read this and not come away with a different perspective on all that's happening in the world today. A must-read!"

—Chris Goff, Award-winning author of *Dark Waters* and *Red Sky*

"A rare gem. Desiderio takes readers on an unforgettable journey where the past and present collide at the very heart of human existence. Flawed, compelling characters and a brilliantly fresh premise make *The Occurrence* a book that will stay with you long after the final page. Sharp, sage, sensational."

—K.J. Howe, International Bestselling Author of *Skyjack*

THE OCCURRENCE

a political thriller

ROBERT DESIDERIO

A POST HILL PRESS BOOK

The Occurrence:
A Political Thriller

ISBN: 978-1-64293-300-0
ISBN (eBook): 978-1-64293-301-7

Cover art by Cody Corcoran
Cover photo "Take Me with You" by Hammad Iqbal
Interior design and composition by Greg Johnson, Textbook Perfect

Post Hill Press
New York • Nashville
posthillpress.com

Published in the United States of America

For Judith

A heart and soul of infinite space and love.

Then. Now. And Always.

Islam claims there are two types of jihad.

The lesser jihad is of the sword; the greater jihad is of the soul.

This story is about the latter.

Abd al Hashim

America, You have committed too many injustices! Our sons have been slain, blood has been shed, and our sacred places defiled. Millions of children have been killed in Iraq though they were guilty of nothing!! To the people of America I say, you will not be safe until your armies quit the land of Muhammad. Until that day, worse than towers falling will you forever see. The wrath of Allah will be upon you again soon.

PART ONE

Up From Buried Light

1

Wednesday, September 9

The desert wasn't the only vast space of loneliness Dominique Valen had traveled—there was the space inside her, the longing to fill the emptiness she had as far back as she could remember. She knew there was more than her insular and hyper-focused world, but she could never shake, and never wanted to shake, the pull of foreign lands and their danger. She knew she was addicted to the adrenaline rush of being close to death. She also knew she was running away from something—from the truth of who she was, for she could never shake the opposite experience either—where she'd imagined herself belonging to a tribe. She'd dreamed of living among nomads in deserts with abilities to heal. It was a rich fantasy life. And while she believed it was a child's fantasy, she believed there was a deeper truth in it. That's why she was here, for almost two years now, sitting in her usual place by the metal-shuttered windows, inside the never-closed American Bar in the Green Zone, Mosul, Iraq, waiting to make her next move—either closer toward death or a healing—to end the loneliness.

That's when the scent of roses drifted in with the morning sun and shocked her from her reverie.

Dominique first smelled roses that weren't there when she was a child. Tuberculosis had brought her close to death when she was three years old in Pittsburgh. But she knew her soul wasn't ready to leave and knew she would survive—because she smelled roses.

Dominique knew the scent of roses was the presence of God. For whenever she'd been in danger it had come to her and she knew she'd be protected. It was something she'd never told anyone, because she believed she didn't deserve it. That the roses came to her now, deepened her awareness and heightened the buzz that danger was closer than it had been since she'd first set foot in this land. It also reminded her that what had almost taken her life, as a child, had branded her with wanderlust and daring, and birthed in her the courage to use her pen as a fearless sword to speak truth to power. That was a confidence hard to shake. So was the fact that she believed she was a fraud. But now, at thirty-three, and as comfortable on a fashion runway as in a foxhole, she was one of the most magnetic and respected journalists in the world. So, she must've been doing something right all these years. Her life had been a pinball machine, blasting from one corner of the world, and her mind, to the other. Writing and alcohol helped ease the paradox. And the pain.

She'd just sent her latest piece to *The Washington Post* and ordered a vodka tonic in a martini glass to celebrate. She knew the American military didn't appreciate getting raked over her Pulitzer-Prized, journalistic coals, but that had never stopped her from telling the truth. Those coals also inflamed the White House when she began reporting they needed to take ISIS's new leader, Abd al Hashim, as serious as fucking plague. His education and innate acumen to manipulate people and situations was just the tip of his violent extremism. They'd made the same miscalculation with bin Laden in the beginning, funding him against the Russians, thinking they could control him. Did they want to lose the war *and their soul* with this guy?

She leaned her elbows on the table, the bartender mixing her drink, just as Julian Ledge pushed open the steel bar doors. He strode toward her, past the white plastic tables filled with Green Zone archetypes: broad-shouldered security contractors with dates in tight tops and high heels, a handful of diplomats in blazers, a construction worker wearing a fishing vest that read *Baghdaddy*.

Julian's rough, handsome face lit with an infectious smile when he saw Dominique. But she knew the ravages of battle had scarred him, and coarsened a heart struggling to reach out. Still, she had affection for him; affection she never could articulate from her isolated realm. But she trembled with the thought that those walls were about to come down.

The bartender—a burned-out local—placed Dominique's vodka tonic on the *Trust Me, I Love Iraq* coaster in front of her.

Julian eyed the martini glass. "Just sent your piece to the *Post*, huh?"

Dominique managed a bitter-sweet smile and sipped the drink while the bartender handed Julian his regular—a bottle of Sanabel Lager.

"I heard about your brother and the other journalists," Julian said.

She'd been at the thin line that separated life from death so many times, she fought against becoming hardened down to someone she didn't recognize. But that protective shell couldn't hold back her anger.

"We all know the fucking risks."

"That's pretty hard."

"I don't need a humanity lesson," she said, her fist tensed. "He was one of ten journalists Hashim slaughtered."

"So. You have no plans to leave here, I suspect."

"Not by a long shot."

"We're each here for our own reasons," Julian said, and raised the bottle of lager.

"To Philip. And the ten."

Dominique bowed her head in love and respect.

"They sent him back to Pittsburgh in a body bag three days ago."

Julian settled into the chair next to her. He kissed the tears on her cheek.

Thunder exploded like a roadside bomb.

She took Julian's hand, and they moved out of the bar through the rain, to the hotel across the alley.

The thunderstorm subsided, but the rain's drumbeat enveloped the hotel room. Dominique and Julian lay in bed. She surprised herself when she told him she loved the rain. How it quieted her and got her in touch with her soul. In the year they'd been sleeping together she'd never talked about her soul. She knew it was foolish now, but something about smelling the roses, in the middle of a war zone, had rocked her as much as it warned her. She turned away.

He turned her back to him, his body taut and electric. He slid on top of her and entered her again. This was his answer to everything—take charge, penetrate, avoid any deeper intimacy.

She used his body to escape, too.

A short time later, Julian had fallen asleep, but Dominique's eyes were wide open. And as the late afternoon sun pressed its way through the curtains, thoughts of her brother and the other journalists jackhammered in her mind. She wanted now, more than ever, to get inside the head of the man who'd orchestrated the executions. That's why she'd been in Iraq for almost two years. Fuck the healing. She wanted to put Hashim in her journalist crosshairs, to know what made him tick, and help take him down. Rage overwhelmed her. She screamed at a God who allowed all this horror, shocking Julian out of his deep sleep.

She screamed again when the balcony doors shattered, spraying shards of glass into the room.

Four dark-skinned men burst in.

Before Julian could grab his Beretta on the nightstand, three of the invaders dragged him naked from the bed and held him down, pummeling his face with their fists.

Dominique watched as one of the men grabbed Julian's pants and shirt and tossed them at him.

Half-conscious and wobbling from the beating, Julian got dressed while one of the men put a gun to his head. Another of the men put a swatch of tape over Julian's mouth, wrapped tape around both of his hands and feet, and jammed a hood over his head.

Dominique catapulted from the bed and clawed her way onto the back of the fourth man, who spun around and slammed her against the wall. She was dazed from the impact, but stood her ground, defiant.

He stared at her naked body. She spit in his face and screamed something in Arabic that infuriated him, and he grabbed her throat.

Pure instinct drove Julian in the direction of Dominique's voice, but he was pistol-whipped across the back of his head and crashed to the floor.

Terrified, Dominique dug her nails into the man's face to break free from his grip, but he rammed her against the wall again.

One of the other men tossed her clothes at her and snapped orders in broken English.

Her hands trembled, as she struggled to dress.

When she was clothed, one of the men put a swatch of tape over her mouth, wrapped tape around both of her hands and feet, and jammed a hood over her head.

She peered through the filthy burlap but only saw shadows.

The next thing she knew, she was being dragged down the stairs and into the fading sunlight, toward the sound of a strained motor running.

She was squeezed into a vehicle with the sweat of men around her, and the press of metal to her side.

Someone was shoved into the vehicle next to her. She knew from his musk that it was Julian.

Dominique shivered as the vehicle crossed into the desert and cold bitter sand seeped inside. She knew this wasn't random. And as strong and defiant as she'd been through the years spent in Iraq, she never fooled herself into thinking this wouldn't be the end game.

She couldn't stop the knot in her stomach from crooking violently.

She retched but nothing came out.

In the foul darkness she thought of the God she'd howled at. And despite her rage at the heavens, she needed to believe she was being protected still.

Dominique wanted to share this with Julian, but the tape on her mouth prevented the words from coming out. If she could speak, what would she say to him? She didn't know.

What did she know? What did all of what she knew matter now?

Sorrow poured through her, and in the swamp of regret she leaned into Julian beside her, and asked God for forgiveness, because she'd never loved, had never given of herself. Life on the edge had precluded others. Now, she was out of time.

The air in the vehicle was thick with the scent of sweat and gunpowder. And in her anguish and regret, the smell of roses cut through her.

2

It was midnight in the Church of Santa Catalina in Cuzco, Peru. The church was built on a revered Inca site called, "Acllahuasi, House of the Chosen Ones." It was built during the seventeenth century to honor women dedicated to working for the Incas, an indigenous tribe dating back to the thirteenth century. Erupting volcanoes and earthquakes could not dissuade the church's founders from honoring these women and the "Virgin of the Remedies."

Religious beliefs ran bone-deep in this land. Handed down for centuries, they gave a resonance impossible to dispute, one reason being that the "Virgen de los Remedios" had inspired a Catholic Order at the end of the twelfth century that proceeded to free slaves from bondage.

Father Manuel entered from the sacristy. He shuffled across the pearl colored floor, dwarfed by Solomonic columns worthy of Bernini, past the magnificent altar of golden cedar still emitting traces of ancient perfume.

Manuel was an old man. A gentle man whose soul vibrated at a frequency that gave him endless, sleepless nights. He walked the floors of his church to meditate on the majesty of God. The solitude and this nearness to his Lord calmed his unsettled yearning to be useful until the day he died.

He was shocked when he saw Jhana-Merise Salva kneeling in front of the carved wooden statue of the Virgin. It was too late for her to be here, and alone.

The young girl held a rose between her praying hands.

Manuel listened.

She whispered the word "*Edubba*."

From his study of ancient texts, he knew it was a Sumerian word meaning: "House of Tablets." But he had no idea what it meant coming from the mouth of one so young. How she knew that word was a mystery.

He waited for her to acknowledge his presence, but she spoke only to the statue with different words now, in a language he *didn't* know.

"Jhana-Merise," he whispered.

But she was in a world of her own.

She placed the rose at the feet of the carved wooden virgin.

He put a hand on her shoulder and a jolt of electricity shot through him. He jerked back.

Jhana-Merise turned—her face beamed with pure radiant light.

"*Nos es Unus*," she said.

"Yes. We are One," Manuel said, excited, acknowledging her words and his internal truth.

Jhana-Merise opened her arms as if welcoming the world—and fainted.

Manuel caught her in his arms and looked up at the statue—expecting it—wanting it to be alive. But the empty wooden eyes of the icon gazed back, as if staring into an unending void.

From the doorway of his daughter's hospital room in Cuzco, Vincente Salva watched Manuel as he prayed over Jhana-Merise, who laid unconscious in bed in Hospital Regionale. An IV dripped fluid into her.

"What happened?" Vincente demanded.

"Jhana-Merise is a special one. *Su hija es especial,*" Manuel answered.

"The doctor said she's in a coma," Vincente said, controlling his anger. He didn't appreciate the priest's singular zeal.

Manuel moved to Vincente.

"Senor Salva. *Nos es Unus. Nos es Unus.* We are One."

Vincente stopped the priest with a raised hand. It was a hand that had laid a thousand bricks, and now worked the coffee fields.

"What happened in the church?" He ordered the priest to tell him.

"She was speaking to the statue of the Blessed Virgin."

"What are you talking about?"

"She was talking to the Blessed Virgin, and the Holy Mother touched her."

"What do you mean touched her?" Vincente said, grabbing Manuel's arm.

"Your daughter is a special one."

"Get out," Vincente snapped, and released Manuel from his grasp.

"*Nos es Unus. Nos es Unus.*" Manuel blessed him with the sign of the cross and hastened out of the room.

Vincente went to his daughter and sat by her side.

He stared at the crucifix that hung over the bed. Since his wife's death he had a conflicted relationship with the man on the cross.

Vincente's sister, Teresa, entered. Younger and not jaded by the world like her brother, she held the hope of religion's promise.

"What did you say to Father Manuel that had him rushing out of the room?"

"I told him to get out."

"He's not the simple man you want him to be, Vincente. He knows the power of God."

Unmoved by her plea, Vincente said, "What else did the doctor say about Jhana-Merise?"

"They're going to do some tests."

"What kinds of tests?"

"He said it could be a type of juvenile diabetes."

"Diabetes?"

"Yes."

"How is she in a coma, then?"

"The doctor said it could happen."

Guilt darkened his eyes. He turned away.

"This isn't your fault, brother."

"She snuck out of the house again. What can I do? Lock her in her room?"

He was in turmoil. And his sister's empathy wasn't enough. Nothing was.

She'd comforted him when he'd lost his wife to cancer, and as hard as she'd tried, he refused to let her help him hold onto his faith. It had vanished with his wife's death. Now his only child lay in bed, unconscious, and he had nothing but guilt and rage to cling to.

Vincente had accepted Christ because his wife had demanded it for their daughter. But after her death he discarded what he called a "useless devotion."

"Thank you for coming, Teresa, but I want to be alone with my daughter. We'll talk tomorrow."

Teresa gave her brother a hug before leaving.

Vincente stifled the panic rising in him—keeping his tears, and his fury at God contained.

3

Eric Vickers didn't like playing with others. He was the new Director of Science and Technology at the CIA, and knew he had a lot to prove. He wasn't good at restraint at one a.m. It was morning in Mosul, but the middle of the night at CIA Headquarters in Langley, Virginia. He stared, restless, pondering the drawings on his desk. He had the responsibility to find Dominique and Julian, and didn't appreciate being schooled in the psychic art of remote viewing by the solemn Dr. Adrien Kurt, who stood over him like a sentinel.

"Why are you fighting me on this, Eric?" Kurt said, as Vickers focused on the sketches of a large warehouse and the well-executed drawings of three faces: Julian Ledge, Dominique Valen, and Abd al Hashim.

"I trust you're aware Catherine Book's 'psychic ability' has given her a ton of blowback," Vickers smirked.

"I trust you haven't forgotten about the shitstorm between her and the agency over the famous WMD incident that gave cause for the war on terror," Kurt shot back.

She'd reported seeing no weapons of mass destruction in Iraq, but there were those who wanted to see it otherwise.

Vickers didn't want to get into any more of a pissing match. A match he knew he'd lose, because Kurt had the ear of the president and Vickers didn't.

"I'm not as naive as you may think, Doctor Kurt."

"But you don't know what you don't know, Eric."

"I know remote viewing was cultivated from a decades-old, multimillion-dollar US government research project."

He needed Kurt to know what he knew, and bullet-pointed that knowledge.

"I know in 1972 we learned that the Czechs, Chinese, Soviets, Germans, Israelis, and British were involved in the study of various aspects of what you call paranormal. I call it paranoia."

"I didn't mean to insult you, Eric."

"I know people like Book claim to see people, places, and things separate, and far from their immediate reality. And I know our backs are against a wall, and the fact you're here proves someone higher up believes the truth is out there."

He picked up the remote view drawing of a battered Soviet Jeep, and the numbers on the side of it. It was the Jeep Catherine had seen the hostages in.

Vickers had sent those numbers to the Intel guys with the hope of tracking the Jeep. Find the Jeep. Find the Americans. Find Hashim.

Vickers shook his head and tossed the drawing back on the desk.

"Visualizing something thousands of miles away is not my idea of good science."

"You're lucky PSYOPs is still willing to work with you guys."

The phone on the desk rang, putting their conflict on hold.

Vickers clicked on the speaker.

"Yeah," he answered.

The agent on the other end spoke with urgency.

"They found the warehouse, sir."

"And..."

"The numbers on the Jeep brought us to a source in Baghdad. That source confirmed its destination. But I just talked to the Pentagon, and Hashim is about to kill Julian and the reporter. The Pentagon sent in a rescue team, but they won't get there in time."

Vickers and Kurt stood there—powerless to prevent the coming slaughter.

4

The abandoned warehouse in the desert loomed large as the Soviet-made Jeep braked hard. Sand swirled.

The insurgents yanked Julian and Dominique out of the vehicle.

Hands and feet still bound, Dominique faltered and banged into the walls, close on each side, as she was shoved through the narrow passage. She heard Julian being dragged on the ground behind her.

She heard the faint echo of Arabic being spoken, as they were brought into a large, empty space and slammed into metal chairs.

This was the consequence of the choices she'd made. Knowing she walked a razor's edge between life and death was one thing. Being about to die was a whole other reality. That reality inched closer when sandy footsteps shuffled over the ground and someone stood in front of her.

They untied her hood, pulled it off, and ripped the tape from her mouth. It tore her skin, and cut her lip. She wanted to scream, but needed air more, and gulped it in.

Her eyes adjusted to the dim light.

A bearded man in white cleric's robes stared down at her—his face sculpted and forged by atrocities and the desert sun.

She recognized Abd al Hashim.

The ISIS leader had serpent eyes, which gave off a fury that pulled her into them as much as they repelled her.

She'd heard that one's life flashed before their eyes at the moment of death. Hers didn't. Instead, her mind flooded with the history she'd compiled of Hashim's life. The paradox of it. He was a shy and courteous child, more courteous than the average. As opposed to bin Laden, Hashim grew up poor, and according to the few locals who had been willing to talk with her, poverty was central to fueling his passion for equality. And violence was the quickest way to be heard. That's when she'd discovered rumors that maybe oil wasn't all of what had attracted those who wanted to conquer Iraq, and what their leaders had been so fierce in protecting through jihad.

She'd been told of artifacts Hashim was said to be hiding in the desert, protected by the Djinn—spirits who lived in places not inhabited by man. While many denied their existence, their origins could be traced to the written words in the Qur'an, and the spoken words of the Sunnah, a verbal record of the teachings passed down from the prophet Muhammad. No one knew where these artifacts were. And perhaps they were just lore. But they were said to contain sacred information. She'd not believed these fringe creeds, but had held onto enough of their possibilities that she left space in her mind to consider them at some point in the future. There was no longer that future. And so what once had occupied the edges of her mind crept closer, as the sacred replaced the reality of what was coming down.

A teenage boy Hashim motioned to, slid in close by his side. Hashim called him Nazir.

Nazir was slim and strong, with luminous skin, like rich earth, and clear intelligent eyes. Dominique thought if jihad was attracting young men this sensitive, it meant there was much more to fear than anyone could imagine.

She watched Hashim rip the hood off Julian's head.

His face was swollen and bloodied, but she could see he was calm, and she studied Julian as his eyes scoped the situation.

Her eyes followed his, and landed on something in the middle of the blood-soaked, sandy floor: a camcorder on a tripod. Hashim ripped the tape off Julian's mouth.

"Hashim. Let her go. Make your point with me."

"My point is larger than you, Captain Ledge. It's larger than your war." The leader spoke with a slight British accent.

Hashim stared at Julian, then nodded to the wiry insurgent close by who grabbed Dominique, dragged her to the middle of the room, and slammed her to her knees in the sand.

She looked around, trembling.

All the men stared at her.

She stared back, but lingered on Nazir, who turned away from her penetrating gaze.

"Hashim, listen to me—" Julian began.

"No," Hashim said with quiet rage. "No."

Dominique turned her head toward Hashim. He moved to her, and looked down into her eyes.

He radiated a darkness of which the devil would be proud. It was one thing for her to hear about him, or see footage of his dispatches and accusations, but to be in his presence was to be faced with an abyss. Still, in the midst of her terror, she wanted to know what made him tick.

"Why?" she asked.

"I could ask the same of you, Miss Valen,"

"This is madness, you must know that," she said in a voice that belied her dread.

"The world is mad, Miss Valen. And we must meet the world where it is."

"So, this will never end?"

"Not so long as there is breath in us."

He sounded like a philosopher, not someone who drew tens of thousands to his barbarity. But it was that intelligence that had attracted so many to his cause. He'd made those who followed him feel like they belonged.

"Do you not know love?" It was the last thing she ever expected she would say.

"Do you, Miss Valen?" Hashim answered.

"Not until now."

She'd caught him off-guard with this exchange.

"It's too late for this," Hashim said.

He commanded the wiry insurgent.

The man grabbed her by the hair and put a handsaw to her neck.

The metal gripped her skin, its razor-sharp points toyed with her mortality.

She'd wished she'd known love before now. It was an ineffable experience to be flooded with that before she was about to die. And with that, she made her peace with death. Her life had run out of time.

As the teeth of the blade were about to tear into her soft skin, and remove her head from her body, Julian broke free and hurled himself at Hashim.

The insurgents swarmed like locusts.

5

The wall of televisions in the Command Room of the Pentagon blasted the internet feed Hashim had set up to broadcast the beheadings. The shocked Pentagon personnel stood transfixed at the screens in helpless disbelief. They were in a bunker, so no one could tell that the sun was rising outside.

Senator Paul Ledge stared at one of the screens transmitting the live images. He watched his son, Julian, battered and dragged back by the insurgents from his attempt to save Dominique.

The imperious Secretary of Defense, Charles Bruton, strode through the room to Ledge.

"I'm sorry, senator. The information the CIA gave us about the location of the warehouse, we'll never get there in time. We've got to turn our attention to the bigger picture."

The senator grabbed Bruton's arm.

"What about the drone? You warned Hashim we'd take out his village if he killed them."

"We've made good on that, senator, but it won't save your son."

Senator Ledge turned back to the computer screen as the feed from the warehouse went dead.

The senator closed his eyes and looked deep inside himself. For all the flesh, bone, and blood he was made of, he hadn't felt much like a human being. The thought that seared into his crippled heart—he hadn't told his son he loved him in a long time.

The emergency phone rang. Bruton grabbed it.

Something unfathomable had occurred. The one reason the soldier in charge of the drone on the other end of the phone could give was that it had malfunctioned. The drone was now heading toward the coordinates of the warehouse, and he'd lost control of it. He tried to have the drone detonated, but the destruct signal didn't respond either, and locked him out from having any effect on destroying it midair.

"Who the fuck has control of it?" he screamed to the soldier on the other end of the phone.

Bruton was in shock that something this cataclysmic went wrong.

The feed from the warehouse came back online.

They all saw that Dominique and Julian were still alive. But they wouldn't be for long.

6

An old man made his way through the winding streets of brick and mortar homes nestled into the hillside in an Iraqi village on the Tigris River.

Hashim's grandfather, Qadir, had lived his whole life in this village where his grandson was born. The serenity of the land made it look harmless, but this town had cultivated a murderer of global proportions.

Qadir reached the town square when the sound broke through the air. He knew the eerie high-pitched hum, he'd been through it before. But there was something different about this sound.

Villagers spilled out from their homes and scattered.

Qadir remained calm and defiant, as he watched the speck against the purple sky grow close, daring it to kill him.

But something strange happened.

Qadir watched the drone make a long sweeping arc like a kite caught in a reverse wind, and he smiled. "The Djinn," he said.

And like the Elohim of The Bible, or "those who came from the sky," the Djinn were the spirits in the land of Allah. Qadir had always felt protected by them, even in the face of the destruction his grandson had wrought as a result of his misreading of the holy text.

Qadir felt sorrow at the road Hashim had taken, but there were more things at work than what he could know.

He watched as the drone ricocheted away from their little village and disappeared into the sky.

7

Two of the insurgents dragged Julian's broken body next to Dominique in the middle of the blood red, sandy floor, as Hashim resumed the televised execution.

Dominique wanted to say something to Julian, but his swollen eyes were searching elsewhere.

That's when she heard the sound.

They all froze at the metallic screech.

The jihadists panicked. Hashim tried to calm them, but they ran for cover, leaving the Americans unguarded.

Julian called to Dominique to follow him and move to a corner of the room. They scrambled as best they could.

From beneath the sand, something jagged jumped into Dominique's hand as she reached the wall and pressed close to Julian.

She let the sand slip through her fingers, uncovering a sharp fragment of stone carved with symbols. It throbbed in her palm.

The screech shattered the air.

The drone plunged through the warehouse roof and sent a concussion through the building, rocking walls, and blasting out the remains of the already half-broken windows.

Crouched in the corner of the room next to Julian, Dominique stared at the artifact in her hand.

The air filled with dust like fire.

Dominique remembered reading of the deaths of desert armies engulfed in simooms like blood rain. Sandstorms, which blotted out the horizon, and sheets of death that engulfed all living things.

She was unable to look away from a tornado of sunlight emerging from the dust and smoke.

They were all unable to look away.

A sound penetrated into her, and her heart pulsed in rhythm with the air.

There was no space between her and the energy that had entered the warehouse.

When the air cleared, Dominique saw all the insurgents were dead—all except for Hashim and Nazir. She also saw that she and Julian were no longer bound. She looked down at the fragment of stone in her hand. It was glowing.

The ground beneath them began to cave.

Hashim held on to Nazir and reached out his hand to Julian, who struggled to stand.

Dominique saw Julian's eyes fire with all the reasons to not reach back.

In the flicker of Julian's doubt Hashim reached out to Dominique.

She grabbed Hashim's hand, and the ground stopped opening. And in that instant she saw the same glowing symbols etched in the air that were carved into the stone in her hand. She saw Hashim see something, too. She watched him watch something invisible flying in the air, and saw him stare at his hand, as if that something had landed there.

She saw Nazir stare out in terrified rapture. He was nodding, as if responding to a voice.

She saw Julian's bloodied eyes go white and sightless, as if what he saw had blinded him.

Then, she saw that they were all holding hands.

The sunlight disappeared as if vacuumed into the air.

Darkness came and thunder erupted.

An aftershock rumbled through the warehouse.

The walls crumbled.

Mustering all the strength he had, Julian yanked Dominique away from the falling mass of stone.

She saw Hashim help a wounded Nazir through the ruins and out through a narrow hall.

She watched Julian struggle to get his bearings.

He reached back to her and guided her through a breach in the wall.

8

Vincente had fallen asleep in a chair in his daughter's hospital room. A warm breeze blew in through the opened window as morning light slipped its way in through vanishing night. Beneath Vincente's hard exterior was a wounded heart that hid against the demands of everyday life. He'd wanted to leave his home since a young boy, but his father needed him to remain and help build homes for others. He could never find a way to tell his father he wanted to leave, to strike out on his own and explore the world. And so Vincente's dreams died. But he loved his wife, and when his daughter was born he'd found his life had been renewed. To lose her would destroy him. She was his joy.

"Don't worry, I'll be all right, daddy," he heard her say.

He awoke and he looked to the bed. She wasn't there.

He rushed to the door and flung it open.

Nurse Arama Chavez was about to enter.

"Where's my daughter?"

"It's all right, Mister Salva. They took her for tests."

"More tests? Why didn't someone wake me?"

"You'd fallen asleep. You've been here all night. I thought it best you rested."

"Where is she?"

"Downstairs with the doctors."

"She's out of the coma?"

"No," Arama said.

"What do you mean, 'no'?"

"Please, Mister Salva. Be calm."

"Show me to my daughter."

She led him out of the room, down colorless halls.

This wasn't the first time his daughter spoke to him when she wasn't there. His wife had been seven months pregnant with Jhana-Merise when he'd first heard his daughter's voice. It had been a warm September morning, his wife asleep in his arms. He'd thought it was his wife talking to him. Her voice was muffled and he couldn't understand the words. *Was she speaking some other language in her sleep?* It wasn't the first time she'd mumbled while dreaming. But he realized this was different, for the voice kept repeating the same phrase. "*Nos es Unus. Nos es Unus.*" He realized it wasn't his wife's voice. It wasn't like any voice he'd known. Maybe he was the one dreaming. But the voice spoke to him again and said, "Don't be afraid, Father. I come with love for all." And while there was no way he could yet know what his unborn daughter's voice would sound like, after the voice came to him again, he knew it was her. He'd never forgotten that sound or those words. And after Jhana-Merise was born, and spoke her first words, there was no doubt it was the same voice. The voice that had called to him from the womb. She was calling to him now.

Vincente paced in the corridor outside the room where they'd taken Jhana-Merise. He stared at Arama who was waiting there. Something about her was familiar.

Yes. She was the nurse when his wife first came in for cancer treatment. Jhana-Merise was with them a few of those times. She was five years old then. He remembered how Arama had developed a friendship with his daughter. It was a connection cut short by his wife's death a few months later. He was struck at how much came back to him of their connection years ago.

He remembered Arama telling him that her mother had died when she was young, too, and how she'd taken on the sole care of her father when her sister left for America.

Strange how much intimacy occurs in tragedy.

"It's good to see you again," he said to Arama.

"It's good to see you, too, Mister Salva. I know Jhana-Merise will be fine."

And as much as he resisted hopefulness, he had hope in the presence of Arama's gentle spirit.

9

The night air was cold. Twilight surrounded Julian and Dominique as they made their way across the Mosul desert. Black smoke rose from the warehouse behind them into the darkening sky.

"We should be dead," Dominique said.

"But we're not," Julian snapped.

He winced in pain from the beating and stumbled.

Dominique reached to support him.

He pushed her away, regaining his balance.

"What the fuck were you trying to prove in there, talking about love? Did you think it would save you?"

"I thought it might save us all."

"That's madness."

"It stopped him, though, didn't it? I know you saw it, too."

"That we didn't die in there doesn't mean we won't out here."

He moved away, unsteady.

"Let me help you."

"I don't need it."

They stood, motionless, in the quiet desert gloaming.

"What happened in there, Julian?"

"I don't know."

"But you saw something."

"What are you talking about?"

"Something happened in there. To all of us."

"We survived. We were lucky."

"It wasn't luck."

"Believe in miracles, if that's what you need."

He continued forward.

She followed him.

Her bare feet gripped into the cold grains of sand making every step a contest of endurance.

To warm her hands she dug them deep into the pockets of her tattered pants. She squeezed the stone anchored there like a talisman. Its pulse, constant in her hand. She believed it had something to do with saving them.

Lights crested over the horizon.

Three vehicles hurtled toward them like beacons from another world. She gripped the stone tighter and prayed.

Julian stood in front of her. Protecting her.

They were vulnerable against a new unknown.

The vehicles grew larger as they got closer. The headlights blinded them.

Gusts of sand, like dervishes, spun upward as the vehicles stopped at close range.

When the haze cleared Dominique saw that they were American Jeeps.

10

Vincente Salva sat with friends in a bar not far from Hospital Regionale. Their daily routine was ten hours harvesting coffee beans, a beer with the boys, and home. He'd not seen his friends in a while. It was good to be with them again. He glanced at his watch. It was later than usual, but he had no one to go home to so he stayed longer, and one beer turned to two and three, because Jhana-Merise was still in a coma, and he was worried and helpless, and the beer calmed him. In that gentle fog his world dimmed away. But the loneliness remained.

The doctors had said her brain activity maintained normal function, which was surprising and wonderful, as they'd also told him it could be dangerous if a comatose patient passed more than a few days in that state. Vincente clung to the good news. He hadn't had much of it in his life.

His buddies were empathetic yet distant. They gave encouragement, but avoided direct mention of his daughter. He wasn't surprised since that had been their reaction when his wife died. These guys weren't schooled in grace or vulnerability. Their lives demanded a hard shell, which was another way he was an outsider in his culture, forced to maintain a macho facade when his soul wanted to give and receive love.

The men turned in unison when Arama walked in the door and trained her focus on Vincente.

"What's happened? Is she out of the coma?" he said, rushing to her.

"No. No. There's been no change. But she's fine."

Vincente's face creased in a thought. If Jhana-Merise was fine, he couldn't figure out what else Arama wanted. Why had she come? He asked if she wanted to join him with his friends. She said that she hoped they might be able to talk alone.

They sat in a corner of a nearby café. A small black and white TV behind the counter played the local news.

Arama spoke of how she believed God had something special in mind for Jhana-Merise.

Her voice soothed Vincente. It cut through the haze of beer.

"Your daughter is a special child of God. I knew that the first time I saw her."

"We're all supposed to be, aren't we? None more special than another?"

"There are some who are more special. It's those we must protect."

"Jhana-Merise is special, but God has nothing to do with it," Vincente said.

Arama told him she wouldn't make an excuse for having a relationship with God. She'd done that enough when she was young. She confessed to her jealousy of having been in the shadow of her older sister, who was deemed the success. But she'd learned to transcend feeling superfluous through the grace of God.

"I used to believe He was merciful and good, too," Vincente said.

"What happened?"

"Life exhausts faith."

He folded his strong, dark hands on his lap. They looked like they were in prayer. He looked down and realized they were. And in spite of his having buried his belief in miracles when he buried his wife, Arama was reaching that pain.

A news story came on the TV.

A report on a shamanic legend from the ruins of Machu Picchu, in the mountains near by.

A local guide spoke of when a sensitive person touched their forehead to the Intihuatana stone at the sacred site, it opened their vision to the spirit world.

Vincente couldn't look at Arama as the report continued. Memories were being stirred.

"We are more than we know," she said.

"I need to get back to the hospital."

He wanted to avoid the emerging intimacy and awareness that he, too, was capable of more than he knew.

11

In the burn unit of the hospital, on a different floor from where she was being treated, Jhana-Merise approached the bedside of a young boy, his burned body swathed in white gauze. His sweet eyes and dark lips showed through the bandages.

"I told you I'd come," she said.

"I believed you," the boy replied.

"You still want to get well?"

The boy nodded.

Jhana-Merise held his shrouded hand.

A subtle light filtered into the room.

The clouds parted to let in a slender stream of moonlight.

"Is the pain gone?" she asked.

The boy nodded.

She unwrapped the piece of bandage from his hand.

He moved his fingers and stared at the healed flesh.

12

Vincente stood at the door to Jhana-Merise's hospital room.
He watched her breathe.
She looked like an angel to him.
But she was still in a coma.

PART TWO

Re-Entry

13

Thursday, September 10

Camp Victory Army Base, Baghdad. The military wasted no time debriefing Dominique and Julian, believing they had vital information regarding Hashim.

They were led into a squat, gray military compound in the Green Zone by more uniformed men than Dominique thought necessary, about to face an interrogation that would have questions Dominique knew would be driven by suspicion. The Defense Department's new guideline was to treat journalists as "unprivileged belligerents."

She and Julian waited alone in the antechamber.

"You're not going to talk miracles in there, are you? That won't be good for either of us," he said.

"I'm not a fool."

"They're going to look for a way to compromise us. Maybe even be suspicious of us abetting Hashim and the kid's escape. I wouldn't hand it to them by saying we held hands."

She knew if she mentioned the stone, or holding the hand of the man who'd executed her brother and wanted her dead, or the sunlight etched with strange script, her credibility would evaporate, and she'd find herself arrested. But what about Julian?

"What did you see that blinded you?" she asked.

He didn't answer.

She pushed it.

"Did you see the words in the sunlight?"

He disappeared into himself. She was unable to talk her way into his silence.

The warehouse was a demarcation between the world she'd known and the one she'd crossed into. She knew Julian had crossed over into something, too.

She knew of mystical experiences. She'd read about them in the aftermath of her near-death when she was young. She was searching for meaning. She'd believed, questioned, doubted, even at times dismissed, that there was something more. Something beyond human reach. But she never could completely deny its existence, even when her memory was desperate to push what had happened to her as a child deep into the recesses of her mind. However slender that thread of experience, it never disappeared. The two others who were saved she knew must be questioning, doubting, and maybe even like Julian, dismissing what had happened. But it did happen. And there was a bond among them she knew she wouldn't be able to shake. It terrified her that once again she'd be alone with no one to believe or share what had happened. But something had.

Julian was calm in his debriefing. He spoke of their luck surviving the blast. No mention of anything else. He said he was ready to rejoin his men in the field but was told by the General his tour of duty was over. The White House insisted.

The CIA agent pressed the matter of Hashim. Julian asserted that Hashim and a young jihadi kid were the only others he saw alive after the blast, and they had escaped. He told the truth, but could see from their skeptical eyes that they sensed there was more to the story.

Dominique couldn't help but be antagonistic to her panel after the impassive General accused her of sympathetic leanings toward the enemy.

"I've spent twenty-three months here trying to understand, to help you mend something that's broken."

The General stared at her.

"I almost lost my life, and you imply I'm unpatriotic because of what I write?"

She pushed back in her chair, breathless. "Fuck you, General," she muttered.

She sat silent, furious about her situation, about what damage this inquisition could do to her career, enraged she even cared about her career in a bullshit moment like this. She wasn't blind to her ambition, or that her fervor had been fueled by the experience in the desert. She knew there were many in the government who didn't like being confronted by a female journalist, especially since their massive stupidity had made Hashim a jihadi rock star.

The General leaned back in his chair, waiting for her to talk. Whatever she planned to say, if anything, wasn't going to be an apology.

14

The miracle of the boy in the burn unit at Hospital Regionale put the town in a religious frenzy.

Vincente listened to Arama speak of how she believed Jhana-Merise had healed the young boy.

"How could she have done that? She's in a coma. Look at her. She can't move."

He begged Arama to say nothing of this nonsense to anyone.

Vincente moved out of Jhana-Merise's room. He didn't want to believe something like that had happened. It frightened him that it might be true.

Vincente understood his culture and its need to believe in saviors. He also knew he needed to protect his daughter from the beliefs of desperate people seeking miracles in place of saving themselves.

Arama came into the hallway.

She and Vincente stood there.

The sounds of the hospital background to their affinity.

"I know you think I'm misguided," he said.

"Your lack of faith is what's misguided."

Those were words like his wife had said to him when she was dying. She believed in miracles. He did too, and prayed for her to get well. It'd consumed him—until she died. That's when he erased all faith from his life. His daughter was the one thing he couldn't deny was a gift from a world beyond the one he knew. And he was frightened that she might die.

He remembered the story of Prometheus ascending to heaven to steal fire from the gods, and bring it down to man. He remembered the story of Jason setting sail to capture the Golden Fleece. He remembered the story of Gilgamesh, the Sumerian king, and his quest to gain immortality. Vincente knew those quests came to bad ends. Was this why he thought of those stories now? Because he feared a bad end?

"I'm sorry," he said to Arama. "My anger is not with you."

"Daddy," a voice called from inside the room.

Vincente turned. He saw his daughter, awake. He rushed to her. Arama followed.

Vincente watched as two doctors finished examining his daughter. The IVs and wires that had been connected to her body had been removed.

The head doctor brought Vincente aside and informed him that he thought she would be all right, but would need to be put through a series of MRIs, and have an electroencephalograph to determine what subtle damage, if any, had been done to her brain during the coma.

Arama escorted the doctors out and closed the door to the room, leaving father and daughter alone.

Jhana-Merise sat up in bed and smiled. She was the picture of health and more beautiful than Vincente had ever seen her. He wanted to ask her about the boy. He wanted to tell her the relatives of the young burn victim were stoking the notion of divine intervention because the boy told them Jhana-Merise had healed him. He wanted to tell her that he and Arama were doing their best to protect her and dispel rumors of a miracle, because he feared the radicalism of belief that grew from such events. Vincente wanted to talk to her about all this, but was afraid. Instead, he reached into the worn denim jacket he wore and took out a pocket-sized, well-used diary.

"You've wanted to talk about your mother with me since she died. What I feel about her, and you, is in there."

Jhana-Merise hugged her father and asked, "You've kept this with you all these years?"

"And read it every night."

"May I have it for a while, father?"

"It's yours."

He handed it to her.

Jhana-Merise held the diary to her heart.

Later that night, Vincente became more frightened for his daughter's safety, when he heard that the rumor of the "Miracle of Cuzco" had spread beyond the town.

He asked Arama where he might find sanctuary for her. Arama told him she had already spoken with the Mother Superior of her parish. She would be happy to offer Jhana-Merise refuge at her convent on the edge of town.

15

Hashim opened his eyes. The perfume of licorice tea and the heat of the afternoon sun warming a bowl of apricots on a weathered windowsill filled him with the heavy scent of childhood. He knew he was in the home of his grandfather. He hadn't been here in years. The bad blood began after Hashim had orchestrated the deaths of a busload of American school children in the name of Allah. It wasn't the Allah his grandfather knew.

Qadir appeared, his hands and face caked with earth from tending the garden.

Hashim watched him wash away the dirt in the basin outside the ochre kitchen walls. He recalled the years he'd lived here and how he'd loved to work with his grandfather along the river in the rice and wheat fields. Fields that have since turned to baked dirt.

Hashim had cherished the old man for giving him an identity. It was a complex identity forged not only by Qadir, but also Hashim's father, whose selfish ambitions had lured his son from this hillside, and immersed him in the evil of cultures of domination and greed. His father's influence had created in Hashim the need to destroy these infidels. It had become easy to believe in the power of destruction, but Hashim had been bled of those opiates since the occurrence in the desert.

Qadir saw his grandson.

Hashim had a softness in his eyes and face. A softness that had disappeared in the years of violence.

"You saw the writing," Qadir said.

"Yes. And the butterfly, grandfather."

Hashim remembered, as a young boy, staring for hours as the insect struggled against the walls of the isolated cocoon hanging from the branch of a date palm tree. He remembered his grandfather told him not to interfere with their birth. If he did, he would cause the creature's death. His eyes were sore from straining to see every movement in this extraordinary act. The silk pad from which the cocoon had hung moved as the chrysalis tore open, and glimpses of color edged into the light. A luminescent multicolored wing stretched through the breach, expanding itself and pushing away on the remains of the shell that still held it within its world.

Hashim saw the butterfly emerge, sit atop the empty casing and expand its dry wings. Magnificent colors lengthened into the sunlight, as if drawing power from its heat. And there within the wings, the same script in Arabic as he had seen written in the sunlight of the warehouse. *Nahn wahid. We are One.*

The newborn lighted like a feather onto young Hashim's hand and looked at him as if it expected something in return. And Hashim heard the same words he heard in the warehouse. The air spoke, "*Nahn wahid.*"

Tears filled Hashim's eyes. He told Qadir of how the sand beneath them had opened and how he saw the butterfly, and reached out to the woman, and they survived.

"You have been devoured by hate."

"What am I to do, grandfather?"

Qadir touched Hashim's face.

Hashim opened his eyes.

He wasn't in his grandfather's house.

His clothes were disheveled and dirty.

A large moon climbed the sky.

He was in a back street of Mosul.

He made his way out of the alley and walked among the people, unnoticed. Head bent. Eyes covered by a nervous hand. The last thing he remembered was getting Nazir home alive.

16

South of the war-torn center of Mosul, in the shadow of the Al-Nabi Yunus Mosque, in a modest home, on a tiny street, in a skintight kitchen with bullet holes and battered concrete walls as a constant reminder of war, Nazir stood, shaking and wounded before his grandmother.

She wore a nutmeg colored headscarf. It softened the wrinkles on her face—a face toughened by the sun, the desert wind, and life.

She applied ointments and a gauze dressing on the wound in her grandson's arm. Shrapnel from the drone had sliced a gash across his bicep. She'd stopped the bleeding. She told him she was concerned with infection now.

The adrenaline from the event still rushed through Nazir, making it impossible to stand still. But his grandmother was strong, and tugged at his waist until he stopped pulsing with energy that made it difficult for her to do her job of healing him.

Her firm yet gentle hands reminded him of how she had cared for him after his parents were killed. She'd left the gashes in the wall as a reminder of the attack that killed her daughter and son-in-law—a reminder for her of the sorrow and uselessness of violence. Nazir had a different take on what it represented.

She placed a hand on his cheek.

"You were spared for a reason, Nazir."

"Yes, grandmother. To continue on."

"Jihad is wrong."

"How many times must I tell you?" he shot back. "Others hear you speak like this it will not be safe."

"You won't bring your parents back with blood."

"No," he said, pressing his opened hands onto the section of wall where they died, "but their voices will rise through the death of our enemies."

"Blood for blood is not God's way."

"Yes it is, Grandma."

He knew she would never stop trying to impart the futility of war, or relinquish her vow to infuse in him the love of all men, which she believed Allah spoke. But after he witnessed his parents' murder, Nazir had been on a different course, following a different reading of that love.

But the occurrence in the desert, and being with his grandmother, who had given him nothing but love, flushed him with an awareness he didn't want to have. That maybe life wasn't as black and white as he believed. He wondered if she could see the sudden conflict in his eyes.

He turned away, and grabbed the shirt she'd placed for him on the back of the rocking chair.

"Nazir," she said, in a voice sweet and gentle.

He turned back to her.

He saw sorrow in her eyes, sorrow he'd seen reflected there most of his life. But it was a sorrow that held love. The paradox terrified and moved him. She'd never backed away from expressing what she believed—that even through grief we must know we are loved and can love in return.

He'd strong-armed his heart against that love for so long in order to survive, but his grandmother's devotion reached deep into that heart. And, it terrified him.

Nazir walked through the busy night streets of Mosul in hopes of finding Hashim. A new world had exploded inside him, a world at odds with the young man he'd forced himself to become.

Hashim had trained him well. Trained him to question and to think. But question and think within the world of jihad. That process fed his dreams, and those dreams fed his reality: a mysticism that served violent ends. He was a mujahid, a soldier to jihad. Allah's undying vessel. And jihad had begun with the Djinn.

His grandmother knew all about the Djinn. But she'd told him another side of those stories when he was a boy—of these mystical creatures who were *virtuous* in the sight of Allah. Male and female, equal in every respect, one no greater than the other. She'd kept that belief from all but him, for she knew it went against the core creed that jihad was born of the Djinn.

She also knew Nazir's heart was good, and that he would one day understand the truth of how love, not hate, was the irreplaceable center of their theology.

17

Hashim gazed into the mirror in the basement of an abandoned storehouse on the outskirts of Mosul. It was the place he had taken Nazir when he first began to teach him. They spent many nights here. Hashim saw greatness in the young boy and wanted to instill in him a confidence that would sustain him.

The secret meetings were the beginning of the darkest part of Nazir's trajectory. They were illuminated by Hashim's vision, dominated by the bloated figure of the United States that he was resolved to rupture.

That resolve had become dust, and blew through Hashim's mind now, as quick as the earth he'd scorched.

In that emptiness—heartache.

Hashim had come here from the alley he'd found himself in. The dream with his grandfather had unbolted his memory. And in the mirror, the warm eyes of his dead mother appeared and stared at him.

He knew she'd hated his being sent away by his father to study under the dark cloud of jihad. He knew she had loved him and wanted him to be a good man. He had loved her, too. But his father had been enamored by the power of the shadow. And that's the path Hashim followed.

It broke his mother's heart.

She died soon after Hashim returned from his first jihad in Saudi Arabia. This was another memory unearthed as he looked into the mirror. What his mother feared had become true. The sweet boy he'd been had become a dark savior. But at what cost? He heard her implore him to answer.

Hashim stared at the straight razor in his hand. A litany of sins he once thought were victories now ripped open his mind. And in answer to his mother's haunting memory, he placed the edge of the razor at his throat.

18

The clock struck midnight inside Adana Airport in southern Turkey. A boarding announcement was made for Turkish Airlines, Flight 1269 to Washington, D.C.

At the sink, in the men's room, across from the gate, Hashim splashed ice-cold water to his clean-shaven face. He was burning up—his forehead hot with fever.

He dried his face with a paper towel.

When an elderly man entered the bathroom, Hashim stood up straight and buttoned the middle button of the dark blue jacket he wore.

Hashim exited the men's room and walked to the attendant taking boarding passes. He took his boarding pass out of his jacket pocket. He was nervous. He wasn't used to not being in control. But it was his choice to be here. His choice to escape.

He closed his eyes and rubbed his forehead. He was dizzy.

"Are you all right, sir?" the young man in line behind him asked.

At first Hashim didn't know the young man had addressed him.

"Are you all right, sir?"

Hashim regained his balance, and turned to the young man. "Yes," he answered, with a smile.

The woman in line before him boarded the plane.

Hashim showed his passport to the attendant. It was a Greek passport. The name on it, Nicolas Sandor.

He handed her the boarding pass. She scanned it and gave it back. He boarded the plane.

Hashim found his seat on the aisle in the last row. The other two passengers had already been seated.

Hashim's eyes went to the elderly woman next to him. He found himself intrigued by the beads she ran through her fingers.

"Such a simple thing can give such peace," she said, when she saw his eyes on her rosary.

"I'm sorry. I didn't mean to—"

"That's all right. They were a gift from a friend. Do you pray?"

He stared at her, unsure what to say.

"Now, I'm sorry. That was too personal a question to ask."

He wasn't sure how much he wanted to engage with her. But his heart beat in a different rhythm now, and had opened a place for strangers.

"Yes. I do pray. Five times a day."

"I love the Qur'an. But I don't understand how…"

"What?"

"I'm sorry, it's not my place."

"Tell me."

He could see she was troubled with what was on her mind. He knew the Qur'an raised many questions. He also saw she knew she could talk with him about it.

"I don't understand the violence that comes in its name."

His answer was a tender question, not an accusation.

"That same violence has also come from readings of the Bible, has it not?"

He saw her take in what he said, and hold her rosary tighter.

"Yes. I'm afraid so." Her voice was quiet and thoughtful. "We all have so much to learn."

The announcement came over the speakers that the doors had been shut and the plane was about to take off.

They each smiled to the other, buckled their seat belts, and went back to their inner lives.

In his relating with her, he'd forgotten he had a fever. But his forehead still burned.

19

Friday, September 11

Julian stood at Dominique's door. Her tiny apartment was in the Mosul Green Zone. It didn't mean insurgents wouldn't send in missiles from time to time. There were no safe zones in war. His rumpled clothes and bloodshot eyes let her see he hadn't slept.

She smelled the booze.

"You need to sober up and take a shower."

She moved back into the apartment.

He followed her inside.

"Got anything to drink?"

"Like you need it."

"I do."

"There's nothing much here in the way of anything. Take a look."

He took in the space.

"Jesus, you're spartan."

She went into the kitchen, and opened the freezer door. The only thing there was a bottle of vodka.

"Anything in these boxes you're packing?" he called from the living room.

"Nothing you'd be interested in."

He rummaged through an open box. It contained books on the Middle East, an Atlas, some small bags of spices, a few pieces of locally made fabrics, a worn copy of the Qur'an.

"You're taking back memories. How quaint."

"Fuck you, too, Julian," she said from the kitchen.

He saw the day's calendar on the living room table.

September 11.

She came back into the room and saw him staring at the calendar.

She raised the glass of vodka she'd brought for him, toasted the memory of that day, took a sip, and handed him the glass. He toasted the memory as well.

"Heard you pissed off General Miles in your debriefing," he said.

"Heard you didn't piss off anyone in yours."

"And they're still sending me back home."

"Your father arrange that?"

"I'd bet on it. I can see it now, the fucker. I have no doubt he's already manipulating my run for senate."

"I'm going back, too," she said, looking for a trace of enthusiasm in his eyes. There was none.

He paced the room with an unsteady gait.

"It might help, you know," she said.

"What's that?"

"To talk about it."

"Shit happens. You never know why."

"I'm not that sure."

"Have you told your boss at *The Post* what happened?"

"No."

"I'll tell you why. Because you know he'd think you're crazy. Fuck. Maybe we are. One thing I learned here. You want to survive? You want to stay sane? You move forward. You move fast. You never look back. And never talk about the weird shit."

"So why are you here?"

He slumped down onto the floor. She put a hand on his shoulder. He rested his head there. The heat from his cheek seeped into her fingers. She wanted him to tell her what he saw in the warehouse. But even alcohol couldn't seem to break him. That didn't stop her.

"What did you see in there?" she asked.

"You're relentless."

"No more than you when you want something."

"And what is it you want, and why is it so fucking important?"

He struggled to stand. The booze played with his equilibrium.

He stared out the dusty, half-opened blinds. The afternoon sun scratched its way across his face. She could see he was debating something.

"You really want to know?" he asked.

"Yes."

He turned to her, as sober as a baby.

"A young girl."

"What?"

"There was a young girl. She got in my line of fire. Came out of nowhere. Her head exploded not five feet from me. Happy?"

He downed the vodka and slammed the glass on the counter, almost breaking it.

She saw he was about to vomit.

"Use the bathroom," she said, and helped him there.

He dashed in, kicked the door shut, and retched.

The staccato of artillery burst like firecrackers in the distance.

She listened to hear if it continued.

It got quiet.

"Hey. You alright in there?"

"I'll take that shower now."

She grabbed the thin bar of soap off the kitchen counter, zipped open her carry-on, grabbed a travel-size bottle of shampoo and knocked on the bathroom door.

"Come on in."

She opened the door.

He was naked, his taut body flecked with scars.

She handed him the shampoo and soap.

"I'll make coffee."

"Thanks. I'll make sure we're on the same flight, if that's okay with you."

"I'd like that."

She left the bathroom and closed the door. How long their connection would last once they landed in D.C. was an unknown for her.

Julian let the spray of water from the shower cleanse him. He was in desperate need of cleansing.

Word came there was no one in the insurgent's house. But he saw movement. What he didn't see was the girl. It was a mistake and it haunted him. Was she pushed into the room? Used as a decoy? He'd never know. For once he'd pulled the trigger and she was blown away, bullets from everywhere rained like thunder.

He'd planted that so far deep inside, he thought he was safe. But whatever happened in the desert brought that young girl back like lightning.

He got out of the shower and looked at himself in the mirror.

"What the fuck are we doing here?"

His tortured eyes reminded him of the men under his command—drunk on the rush of firefights and the nearness of death, and the horror, lack of sleep, and desperate need for forgiveness.

He remembered one of the younger men, Brian Halloway, who was sent stateside after flipping out collecting body parts, blathering that he could feel spirits. Not just around the bodies and shattered pieces of flesh, and not just the Marine dead, but the spirits of all the dead of Iraq. That episode was enough to get him discharged.

He thought of Brian as he looked at himself in the bathroom mirror. He could feel the spirit of the young girl around him and knew he'd never be able to sequester her deep inside him again. He also knew he'd never talk about it again. He had told Dominique, but if she ever brought it up, he'd chalk it up to a bullshit story just to get her off his back.

The truth was, he knew remembering was part of something bigger.

20

It was almost midnight when the government plane landed at Joint Base Andrews, Maryland. Creeping fog and spitting rain made a less-than-warm welcome for Dominique and Julian, jet-lagged and exhausted.

Senator Ledge stared out from the back seat of a government vehicle. He wiped the condensation that formed on the glass as his son and Dominique were escorted from the plane down to a covered area of the tarmac.

Dominique's boss at *The Washington Post,* waited for her under a large doorman's umbrella outside his limo.

Dominique was disappointed when she saw him. She hadn't asked for him to pick her up. She wanted to be with Julian. Maybe it was just that they'd come out of their river of fire alive and that was the intense bond…

But she knew it was more than that. It was something ancient. And she wanted to know what. She had fallen in love with him, broken self and all. She'd never fallen in love. She'd fucked, but love had evaded those beds. She knew his wounds—they were what drew her to him. She was wounded, too. And that he'd talked about what he saw in the warehouse, that he'd talked about the young girl, made her believe what had occurred in the aftermath of the bomb was meant to bring them together. To what, she did not know. But she knew it could heal. And maybe Hashim and the boy he'd called Nazir knew that, too.

Rain thumped on the cover above them. She wrapped a shawl around her head. Julian lifted the collar of his coat to avoid the ripping wind. She slid her hand between the upturned collar and his face and felt his cheek.

"You're burning up," she said, wanting to take care of him.

"I should go. You go home, too. We're both exhausted."

She knew the road back to each other would take time. She knew words went so far.

It would take something more than each other to heal them. Something she'd been looking for, for a long time. Something that always seemed to be out of reach. Something that seemed to be coming in on them.

21

Saturday, September 12

Jhana-Merise woke before dawn in a tiny stone guest room. This was her first morning in the Convent of La Merced ten miles from the center of Cuzco. A painting of Mother Mary hung on the wall over the stiff wooden bed on which she'd spent the night.

She made her way through the ancient vaulted chambers of stone and mortar. Instinct brought her to where she saw Sister Helen greet the other nuns, assembled for morning prayers.

Helen was a young woman—her lucent face bore traces of her Inca ancestors.

Jhana-Merise asked Helen if she might join them. Helen smiled and led her down cold, narrow stone steps, to a dark catacomb with an altar and six pews.

Jhana-Merise's eyes adjusted to the candlelight. The smell of incense and the low hum of the sisters' incantations before they joined in unison filled Jhana-Merise with the longed-for warmth of motherly love.

Thirteen women between thirty and eighty knelt before the altar. Jhana-Merise observed each one. And in turn they each appeared to welcome her with their eyes.

Jhana-Merise saw that some carried sadness, but most seemed serene in their chosen life. She took in these women in long tunics of white, and headpieces of royal blue, and felt safe within these cloistered walls.

The dining room of dark, heavy wood and stone with faded frescoes on the walls from centuries before was familiar to Jhana-Merise. She knew of déjà vu. But this was more than what she knew. This shock of awareness went through her. A vibration, as if she were a string instrument. Some unseen hand brushed across her body. The same trembling she felt when she cured the young boy in the burn unit. The same trembling when she came out of the coma.

Breakfast was spent in silence, yet the curious eyes of the nuns scanned this young visitor.

Jhana-Merise discovered the way to connect in the silence was through a smile, and her openness seemed to melt some of the crusted corners of the curious women.

Later that morning, Jhana-Merise knocked on the opened door to Sister Helen's office. Helen looked up from her reading.

"Jhana-Merise, please, come in."

Jhana-Merise entered. She looked around the room. It was an ascetic space with two wooden chairs, a journeyman's desk, and a handmade crucifix on the wall behind the nun.

"I can't stay," Jhana-Merise said.

"I know."

"Will you help me convince my father?"

"Of what?"

"That he needs to take me to America."

Sister Helen knew this would be the last time she would see her. That Jhana-Merise was young, and youth deserved joy, didn't dissuade her from believing the journey ahead for father and daughter was necessary, and perilous. Helen knew transformation came at great cost. The man on the cross behind her had paid the ultimate price for preaching oneness and love. And, as she looked into the young girl's eyes, she imagined what those who'd been at that man's side might have felt, the sorrow and expectation of helping to birth a new world.

Helen would pray for Jhana-Merise and Vincente's safe passage into their new world.

"Are you afraid?" Sister Helen asked.

"What is there to fear in knowing we're not alone?"

Helen cried.

PART THREE

Convergence

22

Thursday, September 17

Dominique's eyes darted to the walls, the books, the African artifacts in Adrien Kurt's Washington, D.C. office. Anything to avoid his eyes. She was afraid of what she might be compelled to reveal. She was empowered by the experience in the warehouse, emboldened even. She also thought she could be going insane. Would Kurt believe her if she told him about the words written in the sunlight?

She knew he'd worked for the government in some therapeutic capacity before he entered the private sector, but never could find out what that was. And she'd tried. All she could find was that he'd worked with soldiers at Walter Reed, in Maryland. She'd sensed there might be more to that story, but chose not to be a journalist in her own therapy. He was a mystery to her.

For years prior to her tour in Iraq, she'd spent months coming to Kurt once a week for therapy, to work out shit with her family and her own ambitions. But it had been over two years since she'd been back.

And even before she'd left for the Middle East she'd never revealed to him, or anyone, her thoughts of a deeper belief in her destiny—that she could change the world. Not some platitude, but a transformation that accepted evolution as an endless occurring. Not only toward where we may be going, but where we have come from. She wasn't sure what all that meant, but it wouldn't leave her alone. Transformation. Birthing what wasn't before.

The experience in the warehouse, and her implausible connection to Hashim had opened a door to the possibility of being connected to something beyond what she knew. It was something she didn't dare say out loud to him.

Kurt's singular focus drew her deep into that expanse. A connection to something being birthed that wasn't there before.

She glanced at her briefcase on the floor. The stone, a fragment of an ancient cuneiform, was inside. She'd hidden it among her packed things on the army transport plane from Baghdad to Andrews. The writing etched in it she'd been unable to decipher.

"A penny for your thoughts," Kurt said.

She laughed.

"What?"

"So, that's what they're worth?"

Kurt leaned back and smiled. His confidence and gentleness, as well as the mystery surrounding his past, intrigued her and heightened the value and curiosity with which she'd always felt in his presence.

"It must be weird to be back, huh?" he asked.

"A little," she said, meaning *a lot.* She heard the gentle rush of air from the vent, and the soft tick of the clock. She'd forgotten how much it comforted her. This room. This quiet. That had become rare. Hushes made her bristle in war zones. She'd come to embrace the sound of helicopters whooshing against the sky. The clusterfuck of firefights she'd rushed toward, a wild scribe addicted to tracers and phosphorous glow. And that addictive tang of gunpowder. The gifts of living in a war zone. Silence had kept her on pins and needles, not sound. But she allowed the silence to comfort her here.

"How about your friends and folks? How are you doing with them in all this?" Kurt asked.

It was hard to open up the first time back with him, but she needed to talk. That's why she'd forced herself to make the appointment and keep it, despite the scratching of her haunted self to bury it all in an iron clad room of denial.

"I haven't seen my folks yet. Haven't connected with any friends. I told them I need time, they seem good with that."

She watched the afternoon sun drop below the top of the arched window. A stream of light hit her eyes. She adjusted on the sofa to move out of the beam.

"I'll close the blinds."

Kurt got up and drew them shut.

She stared at the clock on the table next to her and watched the second hand move around its face. Tick. Tick. Tick.

She moved to the wall of books and distracted herself by studying the titles. She didn't remember him having such a breadth of literature on the mystical: *Dark Night of the Soul,* by Saint John of the Cross. *The Egyptian and Tibetan Books of the Dead.* And a couple of books by the author Paul Von Ward: *The Soul Genome: Science and Reincarnation, and, Gods, Genes and Consciousness, Nonhuman Intervention in Human History.*

"Jesus."

"What?"

"How many gods do you believe in?"

"It's common after what you went through, Dominique."

"What is?"

"The search for meaning. You've been on that search a long time, even if you won't admit it. You sleeping okay?"

She hadn't been sleeping well. She was exhausted, unable to focus. She hadn't heard from Julian in over a week and that weighed on her.

She took a deep breath and came back to the sofa. She was queasy.

"I've been having dreams."

"You want to tell me about them?"

She rubbed her forehead. She began to sweat.

"You all right?"

"Pieces. They're pieces. I'm being pulled into a…"

She darted to the bathroom down the hall in his office apartment and closed the door.

He heard her vomiting, and moved closer down the hall.

After the sickness seemed to have passed, she was silent for a short time.

"You okay in there?"

"Yeah. I'll be out in a minute."

In the bathroom, she looked at herself in the mirror. Pale. Trembling.

She washed her hands and face, glared at herself, and whispered, "You've got to tell him."

"There are mints in the drawer," he called to her through the door.

She opened a box and popped two mints in her mouth.

She opened the bathroom door and stood there.

"You sure you're alright?"

She took a deep breath and said, "You're going to think I'm crazy."

"If there's one thing I know, it's that you're not crazy. You've been through eons of tragedy, starting with that hospital room in Pittsburgh, up to and including your brother's death, and almost yours."

He led her back into the therapy room.

"What would you think if I told you something came into the warehouse after the bomb hit?"

"I'd think something came in after the bomb hit."

"What if I told you I saw writing on the sunlight that came in from the roof."

"I'd believe you."

"You'd believe me?"

"Yes."

She picked up the empty water glass next to the carafe on the side table. She didn't smoke and needed something to hold onto, in order to stop her hands from shaking.

Her words flowed.

She told him about the ground opening.

Holding Hashim's hand.

The terrified wonder in Nazir's eyes.

"What about Julian?" Kurt asked.

"His eyes went white as if he were blind, and a harsh sorrow flushed through him. I could taste it as much as I tasted the dust."

She didn't tell him about the girl Julian told her he'd killed.

She put the water glass down.

Released from the pressure of holding the glass tight, her fingers came back to life and, like a waking spider, unfurled themselves of the tension.

She picked up the briefcase on the floor by her chair. Opened it and took out a wad of newspaper. She unwrapped the paper. She held out the fragment to Kurt.

He took it and rubbed his fingers around it.

She smelled a faint trace of roses, and wondered if he could. He seemed to have no reaction to the change in the air.

Slivers of light snuck through the blinds and landed on the stone in Kurt's hand. The carved symbols were pronounced in the chiaroscuro light.

"You found this in the warehouse?"

"Yes. And if you didn't think I was crazy before…"

"I don't think you're crazy."

"You will now."

"Why?"

"I believe the stone helped save us."

Kurt sat in his chair, and pointed for her to sit as well.

"How much do you know about cuneiforms?" he asked, looking at the stone in his hand.

"A little."

He gave her back the stone and the light seemed to follow it into her hand.

"Do you know the story of Gilgamesh?" he asked.

"I know it's an early myth."

"In 1872 an engraver of bank notes in London, George Smith, made a discovery. He'd come upon clay tablets in a back room of the British Museum that spoke of man's heritage being far more ancient than had been supposed. The tablets were said to be from the library of tens of thousands of volumes that King Assurbanipal had collected twenty-five centuries before, in the area that's modern-day Iraq. What Smith discovered was these tablets told the story of the '*Epic of Gilgamesh.*' A story of the quest to become human, and the search, and failure, to gain immortality. But what shocked Smith more was that he'd also found himself reading about a flood, an ark, and pairs of animals."

"Genesis."

"No. What he was reading wasn't from the Bible. The tablets he'd found were already centuries old by the time the Genesis we know was supposed to have been written."

"You're saying the Bible plagiarized it?"

"I'm telling you what history suggests."

"And that is?"

"We're more than we know."

"What does this cuneiform have to do with Smith?"

"Nothing directly. But it sets a context. A precedent for what you found. How one thing can open a door to another."

"Do you understand the symbols in the stone?" she asked.

"Yes. The markings refer to an ancient myth from Sumer, a land once called Babylon that's now Iraq."

"Is there anything you don't know?"

"A lot."

"That whole myth is inscribed on that little stone?"

"No. But early language did need to speak volumes in a limited space."

"The first Twitter?"

"You might say that. These markings refer to an inner elevation in consciousness that leads to a place in the world where that level of transcendence exists in physical form. A portal. A split in the veil of reality. But access to it is denied to most."

"Are you saying we experienced a split in that veil in the warehouse?"

"A tremendous force exists where you found this stone. Isn't that what you've accused the government of? That maybe *oil* isn't all of what attracts them there?"

"I wasn't thinking of mysterious portals."

"The Sumer myth also speaks of the Lady of the Roses."

Dominique had never experienced the phenomenon of time being stopped. Time never stopped. It either moved too fast or slow, but never stopped.

But. Time. Had. Stopped.

Her eyes blinked and things moved again.

The ticking of the clock entered her hearing.

"Who are you?" she asked.

"I'm someone who understands what you went through."

"Because you've been through it?"

"Let's leave that for now. This is about you. And you're not crazy. Okay?"

She'd always trusted Kurt, but now sensed he possessed a soul much closer to her own than she ever could've imagined. And, she told him about the sound that came into the warehouse and penetrated her.

"It makes no sense, I know, but…"

"It makes all the sense in the world," he answered. "It's the sound love makes traveling through time."

She stared at him, not clear she heard correctly. "Did you say—"

"Yes. It's the sound love makes traveling through time. Most choose never to hear it."

She wanted to pursue her journalist's drive and get answers to all the questions she had, but wasn't sure she'd be able to comprehend what else he might say, as who he was seemed to lie deeper in the direction she was being led, and at the moment she had all she could handle.

"You'll have your answers in time," he said.

23

Julian made his way through the labyrinth of Walter Reed Medical Center, Bethesda, Maryland. He knew Brian Halloway was there.

Four days without sleep and full-out mania had gotten Halloway sent home handcuffed to a stretcher.

Halloway's breaking point came after he'd watched a sergeant step on a pressure-plate bomb, on a roadside in Fallujah. Julian had ordered his men to collect the body parts in a body bag. But when the bag ripped open on the back of their Ford F-350, and blood and organs slid out like groceries through the bottom of a wet paper bag, the human soup hit Halloway in the face. His knees buckled and he vomited so bad Julian pulled him off duty and sent him to a combat-stress trailer.

After days of no sleep and erratic behavior—Halloway mumbling he could feel the spirits of the dead—he was ordered home.

There was something about the look in Halloway's eyes that had haunted Julian. And when he saw the same look in his own eyes as he stared into the bathroom mirror of Dominique's apartment in Mosul, he wondered if he too was going mad.

Julian stood in the hallway of Mologne House on the grounds of Walter Reed. The servicemen and women here were the crushed and shaken. They convalesced in three-star rooms among chandeliers, and wingback chairs in this curious outpost of the war on terror. They were the lucky ones.

The thick curtains of Halloway's room were drawn and gave it a mid-afternoon melancholia.

Halloway sat in a chair facing the darkness.

The doctor's defeated smile let Julian know there was little help for the man he was here to see.

Julian entered the room, alone. He stood next to Halloway.

Halloway turned and looked up.

Tears flooded his eyes, and a huge smile lit his savaged face, when he saw Julian. It was recognition, not madness, because the first words Halloway said were, "I know why you're here."

Halloway knelt down by his bedside and pulled out his duffel. He unzipped it, dipped his hand into the bag and pulled out a ragged notebook. Sand dripped from it. He stared at the grains on his pant leg and studied them as if he were reading a map.

Julian watched.

Halloway took loose pieces of paper out of the notebook. He came back to Julian and handed him the papers.

What Julian saw scribbled out in a childlike manner in crayon were drawings of tornados of sunlight swirling in slashes of gray dots and black smoke, just like what Julian had seen in the warehouse after the explosion.

Halloway stared at Julian.

"You saw it, too?" Julian asked.

"Yes," Halloway answered in a soft exhale of disquiet and release. It was as if he'd been holding his breath since the roadside bomb. His face and muscles relaxed as he told Julian of the swirling light and the smell of roses that happened to him that day in Fallujah.

He'd feared telling anyone anything after he'd claimed to feel the spirits of the dead, so had chosen the path of silence—the agreed-on path in the collateral damage of war. Whatever trauma Halloway had demonstrated, which led him here, disappeared in the clarity of his eyes, and the force of his voice as he related to Julian, who understood why Halloway had chosen this path. Julian had done the same in the aftermath of the occurrence in the desert—he, too, had chosen evasion.

Halloway grabbed Julian's hand. "We're not crazy, man. We're not crazy."

That he wanted to believe a man in a locked-down ward, more than he'd allowed himself to believe Dominique, was crazy. But Halloway was one of his men, one of his tribe of warriors. That bond was deep.

And as the two men held each other's gaze, Julian saw the clarity in Halloway's eyes replaced by the collateral haze of war that seemed to never leave a soldier's psyche. And Julian knew—some were capable of handling the mysteries of life better than others. This brave young soldier was safer inside these walls, at least for now.

24

Friday, September 18

The Welcome Home party Julian's father threw at a posh Georgetown restaurant was filled with friends and political movers and shakers. But unease plagued Senator Ledge's mind as he watched Julian's fourth martini slosh through his son's fingers. The senator was all too used to this scene, since he'd spent a lifetime watching his wife steady her drinks.

Despite his unease, the senator saw good things on the political front for his son, and knew now was the time to strike. But he was rattled because of what happened to Julian in the warehouse. He knew it went deeper than Julian had let on, and was playing havoc with Julian's mind.

Ledge had private information that a fellow senator was about to be brought up on charges for illegal actions, and wanted to use the opportunity to open a space for Julian to make a run for that seat.

The fact he was a war hero, and his father House Whip made it a sure thing his name would be top of the list.

Ledge and Brent Samuels, a high-powered political consultant, watched Julian charm the wife of one of Ledge's largest contributors.

Martha Ledge wobbled to her husband when she saw him with Samuels. She had a drink in her hand. She always did.

"I don't know, Paul. It may be too soon. You don't want to push him into this," Samuels said.

"Don't hold tonight against him. He's celebrating."

"You sure that's all it is?"

"What's that supposed to mean?" Martha slurred. "Our son is not one of the weak ones."

"All right," Samuels said. "We'll see. Silver Star. Ivy League. It could come in handy with Senator Mills set to implode. Have Julian see me in a few days. We'll talk."

And with that Samuels left.

"Have you even spoken to Julian about this, or have you just decided to use him to your advantage?" Martha's voice was loud, and her face liquor-red.

"Would you even give a shit?" Ledge hissed.

Martha turned away and grabbed another drink the waiter offered her.

Across the room, Julian grabbed another drink, too, raising the glass to his father and giving him the finger.

The senator helped Julian to the waiting limo. He opened the rear door and was about to guide his son inside when fog filtered down from the lamppost light and pulled Julian's attention.

Julian stared at the swirling mist.

"What are you looking at, son?"

Julian was transfixed.

"Julian, what is it?"

"It's just fucking fog."

Julian shoved his father away and crawled into the back seat of the limo.

25

Sunday, September 20

Chilled deep under his skin and drenched in sweat, Julian woke in the room he'd grown up in. The nightmares wouldn't stop no matter how much he tried to numb them.

The young girl he'd killed. The blood of innocent children splattered on walls of insurgents' homes. The spilled guts of his own men who thought too long before they fired.

Julian forced himself out of bed and fortified himself with pills he'd brought back. Pills a buddy had told him to keep for the battles that would rear their heads stateside. The blues, whites, yellows, and reds that quelled the panic. Panic he couldn't strong-arm like he'd been able to before the warehouse.

The ice-cold shower shocked him awake. And the pills calmed his mind. He felt weak needing these, but need them he did.

Julian walked through the home of his youth. The deep mahogany of the walls and staircase. Rooms filled with beautiful antiques and fabrics his mother had chosen in her few moments of happiness. They all held memories of anger and resentment now. The agonizing battles his parents had over his father's absences and his mother's drinking. Battles that carved psychic scars, and drove him into isolation as a child. Until he pleaded to be sent away to school. Away from the grief of living here.

His time at the sprawling campus of Carson Long Military Academy in Pennsylvania prepared him for even more assaults. The kind he'd find in other battles. And he joined the front lines in the war on terror when his father and others had voted to send young men to die. Julian despised their privilege and forsook his own.

Julian entered the den, surprised to see his father there and said, "Thought you'd be at church."

"It's been years," Ledge replied.

Julian went to the bar in a corner of the den and poured himself a scotch.

"Brent Samuels wants to talk with you."

"Not interested."

"You don't even know why."

"I'd have to come from another planet to not know you want me to go into politics. And somehow you convinced him, and who knows who else, the government needs a soldier. I guess my almost getting killed improved my stock, huh?"

Ledge changed his tactic.

"Have you thought about what you want to do, then?"

Julian pressed two fingers into his temples.

"I worry about you."

"I'm fine."

"If you need to talk to someone—"

"I said I'm fine."

Julian turned to leave the room.

"We didn't try to kill you. That's not what we tried to do."

"I know about the 'errant bomb.' Shit happens."

Julian had been steeped in the impossible knot of war. The wondrous acts of courage. The acts of evil. The strange miracles of bombs that didn't go off. The horror of the ones that did. Bullets that missed. Those that didn't. And he wondered if he could ever return to a life beyond that cauldron. He'd mastered the art of defense with an exquisite lethal skill that kept him alive. But a gnawing in his gut had scattered the deck of his life into corners he didn't want to go. He saw a similar helplessness in his father's eyes and sensed they had more in common, but shrugged off the thought.

He walked to the sideboard to pour himself another drink, popping a pill out of his pocket without even checking to see the color.

"How was your visit to Walter Reed?" Ledge asked, surprising Julian, who turned on him and said, "You spying on me?"

"I'm concerned."

"Is there anything you don't stick your fucking fingers in?"

Ledge moved closer to his son.

"I wasn't there when you were young."

Julian raised a hand, a sign to keep his father at a distance.

"I don't need you to make up for it."

But he did. He needed his father and mother, neither of whom had been there for him, to atone for the years of absence in his younger life. But his mother was at the bottom of another bottle in her bedroom upstairs; desperate for the innocence she'd lost. And his father struggled for forgiveness.

"We have no idea what happened to turn that drone around."

"Yeah. Life's full of mysteries," Julian said, as he left the room.

But Ledge lied. He knew why the drone had turned around.

26

Ledge walked into his wife's bedroom. They'd slept in separate rooms for years, and long ago stopped pretending there was any relationship here to salvage.

"Did you tell him?" she asked, standing at the window, a drink in her hand. She answered her own question. "Of course you didn't."

"You're drunk."

"Of course I am."

"What would you have me say to our son?"

She turned to him. Her eyes bloodshot. Her voice on fire.

"Not the truth. That disappeared long ago, when all hell was about to break loose and all you could think of was saving your career. Why change that now? You've perfected lying. But it happened to our son. I knew it would."

"Sins of the father, is that what you're saying?"

"The thing that was a sin was your refusal to believe what happened to you was real. You abandoned a friend you loved to save yourself."

"Jack Dean had his own issues. I wasn't the one to blow his career."

"You knew the truth then, and you know it now. You know what happened when that drone had a mind of its own. And what did you say to Julian? 'You didn't try to kill him? You had no idea what happened'?"

"Yes."

"Why?"

"Because I'm a coward."

"Yes, you are. It's the first honest thing you've said in years."

"Are you going to tell him?"

"That his father also had an experience he didn't know what to do with? Why would I do that? You'd deny it. You could've helped him. But you destroyed that years ago. He doesn't need you now. You made certain of that. So, don't try to make amends. It's too late."

That truth cut deeper into him.

"For the love of God, what have I done?"

Martha peered at him caught off balance at his sudden vulnerability.

If there was ever a moment that could spark the affection they once had, it was now.

He stepped toward her.

She turned away.

27

Catherine Book commanded attention as she walked through the glistening marble halls, past columns that stood like an army of sentinels in the CIA offices in Langley, Virginia.

Her curves distracted men from the keenness of her mind. A hurdle she'd had to leap all her adult life.

Eric Vickers—whose interest in her ability had heightened in the wake of her finding the Mosul warehouse—accompanied her. She knew he doubted how far her ability could go. She also knew her paranormal talent added to the complexity of how people acted toward her. Jealousy. Snickers. Leers. Vickers was no exception.

Her remote viewing mastery to psychically see things far away had the added intricacy of pulling her close to the event. An occupational hazard she'd worked to keep at a distance as best she could. But she couldn't shake the bond fusing her with the four survivors.

She was called "Sister Spirit" when she was young. Traveled with her family throughout the country, revival tents and all. Some reviled them and called them snake charmers, others came away healed. It was a *Gordian Knot* childhood, put on display to present her uncanny ability to tell the believers not only what they wanted to hear, but to see their future. But it wasn't until she was in her late twenties, working for the U.S. government as a diplomat in Israel, that she discovered she had the rare ability to remote view images at significant distance.

She'd kept this new ability silent—until the government was about to go to war after the 9/11 attacks, and she knew there were no weapons where the administration insisted there were. But she couldn't get anyone to listen to what she saw because those in power had an agenda for war. Her advice had become unwelcome within the halls of power until she was able to locate the warehouse in Mosul. It was a reality the new administration couldn't dismiss.

Vickers handed her a dossier as they made their way into the subterranean area of the CIA. She opened it and the first thing she saw was a photo of Abd al Hashim in a beard and dressed in the white robes and cap of an Islamic cleric.

"Intel says he left Iraq under mysterious circumstances," Vickers said.

"Mysterious?"

"He's disappeared from our radar. According to some intercepted transmissions it seems his own people have no idea where he is either. Those transmissions could be real or a ploy. We need you to find him."

"I'm not making a believer out of you now, am I, Eric?"

"Don't be cocky because you drew a few pictures."

"Not defensive, are we?"

They reached the top security area. Vickers used his key card and punched in the code. Doors whooshed open. Again, they were on the move.

"What about the local cells?" she asked.

"They seem to be as confused by his disappearance as anyone, but something's up."

"And he's still alive?"

"You can't 'see' that with that thing you do?"

"Fuck you, too, Eric."

"Ledge and Valen said they saw Hashim and the young boy alive after the blast."

"Any reason to doubt that?"

"There's reason to doubt everything," he said, moving down the hall to a metal door.

He input a code and the door clicked open, revealing a state-of-the-art video and audio recording room.

For all their skepticism in paranormal science, the government held to the possibility the truth was out there. Whenever they were against a wall they gathered whatever psychic information could be leeched from willing and patriotic minds, and they had a room set up to prove it.

She shook her head.

"What's the problem?" he asked.

"You guys don't listen, do you?"

"What now?"

"I'm willing to go through the ceremony you think you need to prove to everyone here how important you are. But I know Kurt told you all I need is a fucking pen and some paper."

"That's in there too."

"You guys with small hands," she mumbled as she went into the room.

A world-weary tech attached a series of wires to Catherine's temples and wrists. She knew whatever she saw wouldn't be transmitted to a computer, however advanced they believed their technology had gotten. She had refined a way to blur her thoughts when needed.

Catherine's mind began to see images. They materialized as they always had, ever since she was child. Her unbending focus on a name, a face, and a location, meant images emerged that informed and directed her as to what had escaped the quotidian mind.

Right now what emerged was a room and a man. Was it Hashim? She couldn't tell. This man had no beard and wore a suit. But his eyes.

Yes. She knew those eyes, and had the searing recognition it was without doubt Hashim.

She surveyed the room he was in and landed on the name and address of the hotel on the pad of paper on the nightstand next to the bed.

The next thing that happened was the overwhelming impulse to protect him. The traitorous thought locked her in an internal struggle. She knew she needed to give the government something; otherwise they and Vickers would solidify their disbelief in her ability.

She sketched what she saw on the wall of the hotel room. A reproduction of a generic pot of flowers that hung over the bed.

She pulled off the wires attached to her temples and wrists.

Vickers clicked the intercom.

"What the hell are you doing?"

She had no idea what was going on with her, only that Hashim needed refuge. That was the last thing in her mind before she shut it off.

Unsettled, she headed for the door and tried to open it but it was locked.

"Let me out, Eric."

A second later the door clicked open.

Vickers stood there.

"What have you got?"

"This isn't room service."

Vickers pushed past her and entered the room.

Catherine lingered in the hallway, not sure what her next move would be.

Vickers went to the desk and saw the sketch of the pot of flowers.

"She get anything?" the tech guy said to Vickers through the intercom.

"Fucking flowers," Vickers said as he presented the drawing to the camera. "Told you this was bullshit."

The tech looked at the image on his computer screen.

"Eric. I think she gave us something."

"What?"

"I know those flowers."

"What the hell are you talking about?"

"That stupid reprint is in every Holiday Inn. Credit my multiple divorces for that piece of information."

Catherine's body tensed when the tech make that connection.

"As I said, it's bullshit."

"Yeah. But it's the only thing we got. Your call, boss."

"Well, you won't be needing me anymore today, Eric" Catherine said, and moved down the hall.

Rattled, Catherine drove her car out of the CIA parking lot. She knew the unique architecture of her brain expanded the borders of her consciousness. That's what opened her to remote viewing. But it had a cost.

The intense sunlight coming in through the front windshield blinded her. She pulled off to the shoulder of the road.

Her dreams and visions were her primary tools for making sense of the world. They were a gift she'd struggled to embrace in her younger years, for she saw the cheap uses of her ability, and it haunted her until she realized she could define her own relating to it, and saw that it could connect her to the world, not alienate her. She was whole in that connection. But it offered no insight into how to deal with what just occurred—empathy for evil.

Was it the devil who had overtaken her in that room, like it had overtaken her father in those tents where people came to heal? Or was it the Holy Ghost she believed had saved her from loneliness and nihilism? Which hand guided her now?

28

Hashim had been in the Holiday Inn on the edge of D.C. for over a week. He'd been fighting exhaustion since he'd arrived. The fever he'd experienced in Turkey at the airport had come on full-bore and he was taking the last of the antibiotics he'd brought with him.

He'd made no contact with his people at ISIS, either in the Middle East or America. He wasn't sure if he ever would. He knew they were searching for him, dead or alive, with the intent of finding Nazir as well.

He'd left Nazir at his grandmother's home, wounded, with no time to discuss what had happened to them, or his plan to find Dominique and Julian. He wasn't sure how his disappearance would affect Nazir on top of what happened to them in the warehouse. But something had happened there. Something that entwined those who'd been left alive.

He knew about the legend of the stones—artifacts hidden in the desert protected by the Djinn. But he'd never found them, despite the belief he had. Perhaps they were there and saved him in spite of the evil he'd committed. Perhaps they'd saved the four of them, and were leading him now.

He had no explanation for what he was about to do other than an unseen hand was guiding him. A different hand than he'd allowed to lead him before.

He laid back in bed. The dreams of his grandfather, the field of the butterfly, and the eyes of his mother pierced through the fever-haze.

Compulsion had got him on that plane. It was this drive that had him rise to lead jihad and be feared. Instinct and passion had been his elixir. They were what had always saved him. But this was different—needing to find the two Americans he once wanted to kill, because now he needed their forgiveness.

But would it have impact—his crisis of conscience?

He knew the impact of the evil he'd done—the orchestrated acts of terror. The impact of surrender was unknown. He knew the fever was his conscience burning with that choice. And he knew it would let him do nothing but seek forgiveness and surrender. From that there was no turning back.

He went into the bathroom, ran cold water in the sink, and washed his face.

He looked in the mirror and held onto the countertop to steady himself.

He knew he wouldn't make it further without medical help. It was a gamble he'd have to take.

29

Catherine hadn't moved. She was still in her car on the shoulder of the road. She knew whatever choice she made now would determine the rest of her life, and maybe cause her death.

She'd come upon charlatans, and those who had wanted to do her and her family harm. You don't go unscathed when you claim to heal people and often do. Enemies flock to destroy your reputation, if not you. What would happen if anyone found out she'd had empathy for Hashim, and kept what she saw from the CIA?

Wet canvas, sawdust, and kerosene flooded her senses, and sent her back to the tents of her youth. She thought she'd eradicated that past and those traumas of the circuit she was forced on. It took years to stop feeling like a freak. And when she began to realize she could remote view, she took it as a sign to escape the rolling revival she'd been born into. But here and now she was in the midst of a new madness that had nothing to do with the ghosts of her past. Or maybe it had everything to do with it and what she'd been being guided toward all her life. It was madness, but she was overwhelmed with the need to protect Hashim. That's when she flashed on the fact that he was no longer in the hotel, but on his way to George Washington University Hospital.

30

Catherine spotted Hashim sitting in the overcrowded waiting room in the ER. She knew staring would frighten him, and so sat across the room in one of the few empty chairs available and glanced his way. No one else paid him attention.

She could see he was in pain, from the way he rubbed his forehead and wrapped his arms around himself. But there were other more urgent illnesses the staff needed to attend, and so he waited.

The seat next to Hashim freed when a nurse escorted the young woman with bruises on her face sitting next to him out of the waiting room into the inner corridors of the ER.

Catherine picked up a magazine on one of the tables as she made her way to the empty chair and sat next to Hashim.

She looked down at the magazine and saw it was *National Geographic*'s feature cover story on Islam.

The cover photo drew Hashim's attention.

"Would you like to read it?" she asked.

"No, thank you," he answered.

She nodded and flipped through the magazine. But out of the corner of her eye she saw Hashim's hands. They were rubbing each other. She was struck with how sensitive they were. She saw Hashim's awareness of her attention on him and he moved to stand. She reached out to him. Hashim froze.

"I'm not here to harm you," she said.

"Who are you?"

"The CIA knows you were at the hotel. It's a matter of time before they tell the FBI and they track you here."

His eyes darted around the room. She could see he was looking for the quickest way out.

"I know you have no reason to trust me, but I can take you to a safe place."

A nurse's voice called, "Mister Sandor. Mister Nicolas Sandor."

Hashim stared at the nurse, who saw his attention and approached him, asking if he was Mr. Sandor.

Catherine whispered, "If you go in there they will find you."

Overhearing that the nurse said, "Is everything all right?"

Hashim looked to Catherine.

"Would you like to come with me, sir?" the nurse asked.

Hashim hesitated.

The next move was up to him.

"Sir. Would you like to come with me?"

His voice wavered. "I'm feeling better, now."

Confused, the nurse shrugged and said, "Whatever you think best."

He turned to Catherine and said, "You can take me home."

"Well. We're here if you need us," the nurse said.

She looked at her patient chart and called another name as she moved away.

"Who are you? And why are you doing this?" Hashim whispered.

"My name is Catherine Book. And, all I know, is that it's what God wants me to do."

She saw something in his eyes she never expected from one who'd been so ruthless and violent—vulnerability and surrender.

A short time later, FBI agents swooped into the ER.

Vickers had sent artists' renderings of Hashim to the Bureau. Renderings that included all possible manifestations of how he might look. Renderings that had him with a full beard, clean-shaven, heavier than they'd known him to be, and thinner. He also sent them the only thing he had. The drawing of the flowers.

The FBI had emailed the renderings of Hashim to all the Holiday Inns in the surrounding areas. The one on the border of the city responded in the affirmative. But when the agents arrived there, the manager told them the man in the drawings had been taken to George Washington University Hospital.

At the hospital, the agents questioned patients and staff to see if any of them might give information on the couple that had been there and left.

When they showed the photos to the nurse who'd engaged with Hashim, she pointed to the clean-shaven version, and gave them a description of the woman with him.

31

They hadn't met each other. Dominique had reached out to Catherine in the aftermath of what happened in the warehouse, but never got a response. It was hard for Catherine to take acknowledgment for a gift she believed she'd never worked for, or even wanted. Truth was, she got shit for being able to see what she did, and kept it close to her chest unless there was an urgent need. There was now. And she reached out to Dominique.

Catherine stood in the living room of Dominique's modest apartment in Northwest Washington near Logan Circle. It wasn't far from where Dominique worked at *The Washington Post*.

She and Catherine had known about each other through Adrien Kurt. Their connection was cemented by Catherine's guiding the CIA to the warehouse. But this was the first time they'd been face-to-face.

"Where is he now?" Dominique asked, stunned at what Catherine had told her. "Where is he, Catherine?"

Dominique tried to remain calm, but her mind raced with what this could mean.

"He's not here to harm either you or Julian."

"Why is he here?"

"You'll understand when you see him."

"You're asking me to trust you with my life."

"I've already trusted mine to him. Be at this location tonight," she said, handing Dominique a paper with an address. "You and Julian."

"I don't understand what's going on."

"You will."

Dominique looked at the address.

"Virginia Beach?"

"I have a cottage there. You'll be safe. Please trust me. There's something remarkable going on beyond what we're able to comprehend."

Even in her panic, Dominique knew that was true.

32

In the all-white farmhouse country kitchen in Catherine's Virginia Beach cottage, Julian glared at Hashim, who was weak and leaned against the kitchen counter.

Catherine handed him a damp washcloth to wipe the fever-sweat from his forehead.

Dominique watched from the doorway, trusting what she'd said to Julian to get him here, would be the catalyst for him to grip what was happening.

Julian pulled out his revolver and pointed it at Hashim.

Dominique put herself between the two men.

"Are you fucking crazy!" Julian said.

Dominique didn't budge.

Neither did Julian. He was a fighter and would fight until his walls were forced to crumble.

Dominique stared at him until he lowered the gun.

"Okay. You tell me why you're here?"

"I'm here because of the things I've done," Hashim said. "There is no forgiveness unless it comes from Allah."

"Allah's not here, in case you haven't noticed."

"Allah is in all people."

"What the fuck is going on?"

"I came to ask your forgiveness. Both of you,"

"Forgiveness? There's no forgiveness for you."

"Julian. Listen to him," Dominique said.

Julian steeled himself against her plea and didn't take his eyes off Hashim.

"I understand your rage and your doubt."

"You don't understand shit."

"You can call the police. But hear me before you do."

"What could you say that would change my mind to see you as anything but the evil you are?"

"You're right. I don't deserve forgiveness, or to live. But if I do, I promise I will do all I can to bring the caliphate down, because they will get stronger unless someone reveals what they know about them."

Hashim labored to a kitchen chair and sat.

Julian couldn't believe what he was hearing. A week and a half ago Hashim was about to execute them. Now, he was a frail man asking forgiveness, and offering to take down the caliphate.

"Why should we believe anything you say?"

Hashim spoke of his mother. A beautiful soul he'd drifted from in his rise to power. He spoke of his father, how he'd hated those who misused power, possessions and money. It was a powerful drug for a young boy to be mentored to take down the privileged. More powerful than the vulnerability of his mother. He spoke of the veil of forgetfulness that had lifted since their deliverance in the warehouse, which opened him to those buried memories.

"I grew to despise my mother's meekness. It had no place in the world I saw. So, I followed in my father's footsteps. I regret that."

"Those are just words," Julian said.

"I understand."

"More words."

"Make your call, then."

Julian took out his mobile.

"Wait," Dominique said.

"Okay. You tell me what we do now."

"Why won't you get it? Something unfathomable has brought us here. Why won't you see it?"

"Because he murdered thousands of innocent people."

"Our hands are bloodied, too."

"You're comparing us? Fuck you."

He raised his gun into the air.

"Julian. Stop it," Dominique said, and slapped his face.

He was pulled farther across the tightrope he'd been on, deeper into his own conflict with all he'd done, and all that had occurred.

Survival in his world demanded black or white. Hashim had colored it in an unsettling shade of humanity.

Julian refused to believe the game had changed in the warehouse, but it was Hashim, here, now, who ripped a hole in his armor, and it slammed him into the reality that nothing was the same, no matter how much he denied it.

33

Monday, September 21

The airport doors opened and passengers exited the Dulles terminal. Nazir looked liked an American teenager. A couple of days' growth of beard, a gray Patagonia vest. He blended into the melting pot of the twenty-first century as he moved through the crowd carrying a backpack.

He'd never been to America. And now he was in the center of its government. This was the enemy. But as he stared at the crush of people, they didn't look that much different than he. And all the stories of the infidels who lived here seemed just that. Stories to instill rage and righteousness. But he had none of that standing amid the humanity around him.

People who stared at their phones like the youth he knew. Some distracted. Some lost. Some who smiled and hugged those for whom they'd been waiting. Families. Children. Lovers. Loners. They didn't look much like enemies. Perhaps this was part of the transformation that occurred after he survived the blast. But he wasn't sent to see through the rage and righteousness. He was here to hold them in his fist.

Nazir knew the cells were on high alert since Hashim had disappeared, and through their international pipeline were able to track him to Turkish Flight 1269. What they didn't know was why Hashim had come to Washington, if that was indeed his final destination. This was Nazir's job.

Nazir had faced much confusion since the desert occurrence. And after, when Hashim had brought him to his grandmother's home, there was sadness in the cleric's eyes. A sadness that said to Nazir, *this is the last time we may be together.* It was those sorrowful eyes Nazir couldn't shake from his mind.

He spotted a man he recognized from a photo given to him in Mosul. This was his connection.

The man brought him to a waiting car.

34

3511 Massachusetts Avenue was the address of Church Dry Cleaners. It looked like a full-fledged dry cleaning operation, complete with the sharp, high-inducing chemical smell of Picrin, and the whirr of row upon row of plastic covered clothes that swayed overhead like an amusement park ride. It was a front for an ISIS cell.

Nazir watched Imam Sayyid Sarif appear through the rows of hanging clothes.

Sarif took Nazir in his massive arms and gave him a warm welcome. He spoke English and encouraged Nazir to do the same. Nazir told him that his vocabulary was limited, but that Hashim had taught him well, so he could get by in most cases.

"Very good," Sarif replied. "The better we assimilate the more impact we have."

The back room of the cleaners was lit with fluorescents. Its glare made Nazir squint.

Sarif spread out his burly arms as a silent introduction to the three men sitting there, who would help in the hunt for Hashim.

Nazir analyzed these three compatriots. His mind clicked off a series of immediate observations: Arrogant. Undisciplined. Soft.

Although Nazir was the new kid, the crucible of war had formed him, while these men had been overstuffing themselves tending to their "assimilation." Nazir despised that word.

Nazir was an insider with a privileged track into their target's mind. He told the men their first objective must be to find the Marine and the journalist. That would be the quickest way to find Hashim. He didn't know why, but Nazir sensed Hashim was here because of the Americans—and not to do them harm—but kept that to himself.

Sarif's daughter, Mariam, reminded Nazir of home. Though born and educated in America, she looked like every bit of earth he'd come from. Her face warm and rich like desert sand. They spoke in Arabic, which heightened their connection.

She helped Nazir choose a new wardrobe from the clothes her father had brought for him, for his assimilation.

Nazir changed in the small storage area in a back room of the dry cleaner. The door was ajar and Mariam had many questions about his home. Questions Nazir knew her father would never let her ask. But he could see that she'd been lost in America and longed for the land her father so often talked of. And so, he let her defy what was forbidden, and told her about his home, for he was lost here, too.

He told her of his experience on the other side of the world, and she continued to be enthralled and asked questions about his life and family.

The more he talked, the deeper his conflict grew. The words his grandmother had spoken stretched across his thoughts like ticker tape. "Blood for blood is not God's way." She'd said that in the aftermath of his parents' death, and again after the occurrence in the desert. "You were spared for a reason. Jihad is wrong." Nazir had no defense against her words now. But he needed to present the self all here believed him to be.

"Are you all right, Nazir?"

"Yes..." But it was a lie.

What had happened to him shook the core of his belief.

He looked different in his dark blue fitted jeans and crisp, white shirt. But he saw a deeper change beyond the clothes. There was a dark cast of sorrow in his eyes reflected in the glass from which he couldn't turn away. And staring at his reflection it became clear that the reason to find Hashim and facilitate his capture was misguided.

35

The FBI had an informant inside Church Dry Cleaners. His real name was Aaron Ajam, but to the members of the cell he was Mustafa Taliq. He'd been undercover for a year, recommended to Sarif by a member of ISIS here in the states.

Good undercover men come in shades of gray. They're men whose faces you forget. That wasn't Taliq. He thrived on being noticed. Arrogance as camouflage. It's one of the things that kept him alive.

Taliq burned with intensity. But heat this intense burned off in time, and Taliq figured he had another year at most before he'd turn cold and need to come in. Right now he was in the middle of figuring out what Hashim was doing in America. No one inside the terrorist cells or at the FBI had been able to figure out the "why." He wouldn't put it past Hashim to keep certain cells out of the loop, forcing them into confusion in order to get the Bureau caught up in that misdirection while he planned an end run toward another 9/11. Whatever that might be, it would be fierce. Hashim had been responsible for thousands of deaths, so why would he stop? Taliq needed answers. And that this young emissary from across the world had appeared made him hyper-aware something was about to go down, and he was going to insert himself into whatever that was before anyone else.

36

In a local mosque in the center of D.C. Nazir's ambivalence was carving a deeper fracture in his psyche. Prostrate, as his forehead pressed into the prayer rug, he was disturbed by something Taliq had said to him when they met: "Are you afraid to enter paradise?" Had Taliq noticed Nazir's conflict? A mash of thoughts collided as his head pressed harder into the praying floor.

Hashim had told him there were reasons for their survival. Nazir had always thought it was for Allah, though Hashim was never specific with what the reasons were. He'd told Nazir that soon he would come to know. Did Hashim have his own doubts? Why had he left? Nazir tried to stop the thoughts that ran like wild horses in his mind.

A strange lightheadedness overcame him and a voice said, *Protect him. Save him. He will help us all.*

Nazir shuddered.

"You okay?" Taliq asked.

Nazir opened his eyes.

Prayers were over. Everyone was gone except Taliq who watched him, and reached out his hand.

Nazir took it to steady himself.

"Come, my friend," Taliq said, guiding Nazir out of the mosque. "Let's have tea."

Nazir followed. But there was something about Taliq that made him nervous.

In a Starbucks near the mosque Taliq and Nazir sat in comfortable, overstuffed chairs by the window.

Nazir looked at the cup of tea in his hand and spun the sleeve, intrigued by its purpose.

The place was jammed with young people all in various stages of self-conversation: texting, head phones on, listening to music in worlds of their own, or on computers, reading or writing.

Nazir took the sleeve off the cup and slipped it over four of his fingers.

Taliq chuckled. "More interested in that than the tea?"

"It's not very good."

"You expected something like home?" Taliq said with a grin. "I understand. You'll not find much of that here."

Nazir slipped the sleeve off his fingers and back onto the cup. He watched the people outside. A parade of well-dressed men and women. He chuckled and leaned into Taliq.

"Are *you* afraid to enter paradise?"

"I'm sorry if my question disturbed you, Nazir."

"Are you?"

"We shouldn't be talking about this here."

"Look. No one's listening. No one cares."

"We don't have to be friends, brother. We don't even have to like each other. But I'm as concerned as you as to why Hashim has come here. I'd like to help you find him."

"I don't need help."

"Sarif believes you do. You blew off the other three with a wave of judgment, dismissing them before you got to know what they're capable of."

"I don't need to live with them to know what they're capable of."

"Fair enough. But whether you like it or not, Sarif has ordered me to work with you. This 'tea,' as misconstrued an idea as it is, was an attempt to get to know each other a bit."

"Do you know me any more now than you did?"

"I know you speak English much better than I thought you would."

"Thanks for the tea."

Nazir got up and left.

Taliq waited until Nazir was out of sight. He took out a burner phone, dialed a number, and waited until someone answered.

"I made contact," Taliq said. "It's not going to be easy to work together, but Sarif will convince him. I'm sure of it." He ended the call.

He grabbed the two cups of tea off the table and dropped them into the trash bin. His eyes probed the room, as they always did, to make certain no one cared or was suspicious about these two dark men who looked like people they feared. No one did.

37

Catherine was startled awake in the middle of the night. Her connection to Hashim had grabbed her so deep she was being bombarded with images of people and places he'd talked about. She grabbed a sheet of paper and sketched her remote dream.

Nazir had arrived in D.C.

She walked tentatively, across the creaky floorboards on the second floor of her cottage.

She knocked on the door to the room where Hashim slept.

When he opened the door he was dressed. He looked better. The fever had broken.

Catherine showed him the drawing.

"He's arrived?"

"Yes. He's here in Washington."

Hashim stared at her.

"What is it?" she asked.

"How are you so comfortable with me? And why so willing to use your ability, and put yourself in danger?"

"Danger isn't foreign to me."

The gathering awareness of a deeper connection to him was something for which she had no reference.

From the open balcony doors, they looked out at the lake.

Moonlight spread across the ducks gliding over the quiet water. They immersed their iridescent heads beneath the surface, in search of food or whatever other adventure they bobbed for in the dimness of the tow.

He reached into his pocket and took out a piece of paper. He handed it to her.

She opened it and read it to herself. It was written in English.

There are stories we carry inside that have slipped beyond the veil of consciousness and wait until a certain time. And, as a falcon descends upon its prey, we rise up more fierce and hungry than the falcon, through ashes at the merest fraction of light, grasping, trembling for God, in order to heal the desire to destroy.

"You wrote this?"

"When I was a boy."

In the grief of his eyes she saw he was still grasping for that fraction of light.

"Even from the blackest nights there can be salvation," she said, and handed the poem back to him, but he held up his hand.

"Keep it in remembrance of who I once was and want to be again."

He looked at her a long time. She didn't avoid his gaze. A bridge had been created between them.

She held his poem like a prayer in her folded hands.

38

Tuesday, September 22

Her name was Isabel Chavez. She was a lawyer for the Department of Justice and had spent a week in Manhattan beginning to collect data the department would use to prosecute Hashim upon his capture. The agencies were sure they would find him, one way or another. It was still top secret that he was in America. A team of lawyers had been put in place for the trial that would follow. It would be a circus, but they needed to be prepared.

Isabel stared out the plane window, watching the afternoon sun beat down on the ground below as the plane made its approach to Dulles.

The wheels hit the tarmac.

The plane glided to its gate.

First thing Isabel did was turn her mobile back on.

There were text messages, emails and phone calls.

Isabel was startled when the first phone message she heard was from her younger sister. They hadn't talked in months. Isabel listened to the message; afraid it might have something to do with their father. But Arama spoke, eager to tell her sister of the miracle that had happened in Cuzco, how she was called to help the young girl, and how Isabel would play a part.

Called? Miracles? The land of magical thinking. This nonsense was why she'd left Cuzco.

She put her phone down, distracted with the preoccupation that grew inside her. Thoughts of her sister had come in streams in the past week, and she couldn't dismiss the strange charge that had been running through her the past few days.

Isabel was the beauty, the motivated one with the drive to succeed no matter the cost, while Arama was the plain sister, happy to be of service to the poor and forgotten.

But for all her success Isabel wasn't happy. Say what she would about Arama, dismiss her flights of fantasy, her magical thinking, but bottom line—Arama was the one at peace. If Isabel could admit it to herself, Arama had always been at peace.

Had Isabel yearned for the opposite of what she'd strived for? No matter how much she'd left behind and achieved, her sister hovered in the corners of her mind. She hated these doubts, and that she and Arama were, and would forever be, connected. Connected in a way that always pushed Isabel to the edge of some giant unknown. Unknowns she'd fortified herself against with all the might she had, and all the common wisdom in the rules and laws that were on her side—that this physical world was the one provable reality.

39

Vincente Salva hadn't prayed in a long time, yet he was kneeling in the church of La Merced, Cuzco. Relics and remembrances of the impassioned lives of saints and saviors surrounded him. He thought about Jhana-Merise. She was not a saint. She was not a savior. She was a little girl. Yet he knew his mission was to protect her. He knew she was his for a short time. He knew she would never marry, never love another except her God. And this filled him with sorrow, yet he knew it was her destiny. He'd known it from the first time she spoke to him from his wife's womb. He'd hated God for the gift of knowing. He'd hated God for taking his wife. But now on his knees he was asking for help. And as he prayed he realized it wasn't God he'd hated, but the intermediaries who'd claimed to speak for Him, promising things they could never deliver. The ones who wallowed in gory details of sin and crucifixion.

Vincente had studied the lives of saints and kept up with news of visionaries around the world. It was part of his silent vow to know as much as he could to protect his daughter. He knew of the messages from Fatima and those of Medjugorje. Places where young children had claimed to be visited by the Virgin Mother. Places that had become shrines, and the children objects of adoration, and ridicule.

Vincente was familiar with the Madonnas that had appeared in clouds. Or statues that had shed tears of milk, blood, and honey. And now in the new century, the internet had become an instantaneous and integral source of reported apparitions and the sharing of faiths, genuine and otherwise. Through it all he knew there were those who'd cast critical eyes on anyone who challenged their beliefs. And so, he'd surrounded himself with a wealth of learning to inspire, sustain, and ready him for the conflicts he'd always known were ahead.

He remembered how Jhana-Merise had kept to herself during school, and how her fellow students had thought she was strange, but not as strange as they would have thought, had they known her one friend was God.

40

Vincente knocked on Sister Helen's door. She welcomed him into her office.

VIncente stared at the crucifix hanging over the desk behind her. His anger at that symbol had diminished in the days since his daughter came back to life.

Helen told him the marriage had its ups and downs.

He wasn't sure what she meant.

"We're all married to Christ here," she said with a smile. "We nuns."

She showed him the simple wedding band she wore.

"It must be lonely," he said without thinking. "I'm sorry, I didn't mean…"

"It's all right. Yes. It used to be. But I realized I must give myself completely. Doing that, I've found who I am. Oh, there were many dark nights. But they're not the same now."

His hands moved almost against his will, running his fingers through his hair, rubbing his face, his hands, rocking back and forth, uncomfortable with her honesty and connection.

He continued to avoid her gaze.

She sat back in her chair, eyes on Vincente.

"I was surprised when I saw you at the door, Vincente. I wasn't expecting you. Would you like to see Jhana-Merise?"

It had been less than a week since Vincente had seen his daughter. And he missed her.

"What are we going to do?" he asked.

"About your daughter?"

"Yes."

"We'll have to ask her."

"Yes. I suppose you're right."

He rubbed his hands on his thighs.

"You're a good man, Vincente. I hope you know that."

He went to the open window. He saw a family of swallows had made their home in the hollow of the orange tree. Their song dotted the air.

"I thought God had abandoned me. Then Jhana-Merise was born."

He spoke of that September morning when his daughter's voice came to him for the first time, and of the grace that came into their lives with her birth.

"She was born with the scent of roses," he said.

He turned back into the room. For the first time since he'd arrived he looked into Sister Helen's eyes. He cherished the sweet energy flowing from her, and thought how lucky God was to have her as His wife.

"God tests our faith," she said. "The road is not easy, nor simple, but it is a road back to Him. While you may doubt, and fear the journey ahead, you must know you're not alone on the path."

As uncomfortable as it had been at times, he'd learned to talk with women, being the one boy in a family of them. He understood his mother and came to understand her tears. They would talk for hours about life. She wasn't happy married to his father, but ritual died hard, and divorce was worse than living with sorrow in the eyes of the church, so she'd cried instead. And while his own marriage was rocky, their arguments and conversations had kept both of them vital and linked. They'd challenged each other and may not have been perfect together, but his heart ached in his wife's absence.

Through the years he'd been privileged to listen to the female mind. He'd learned to listen when women spoke with passion and intent, although it was one of the first things for which he'd cursed God. That sensitivity didn't go down with the macho boys of his youth.

He cherished being here, in this space of openness and respect.

"Would you like to see your daughter now?"

As she passed him on their way out, he wanted to touch her in gratitude for her gentleness, but he didn't. Instead, he said, "Thank you."

41

Jhana-Merise waited for her father by the olive tree in the convent courtyard. Its trunk gnarled upward and its strong arms reached toward the sky. The sweet pungent flavor of the ripening olive fruit filled the air, and their deep purple color vibrated against the red of the setting sun.

There had always been something in her eyes that reflected a deeper wisdom. She was growing up fast, but he wanted to hold onto the little girl.

He held tight to the flood of love in his heart. He didn't want to overwhelm her.

There were many things he had wanted to tell her, but he didn't want to burden her with his life.

He saw her watching him with gentle grace in the courtyard. The pressure on his heart released and gave him an unfamiliar peace.

She nestled her head into his chest. He folded his arms around her.

"I heard you speak to me before you were born," he said.

She looked up at him, her eyes bright.

"I heard you answer, Daddy."

Perhaps she was a savior, he thought. She'd saved him.

In the intimacy of the late afternoon she told him about her dreams of two sisters, and how a voice spoke to her and said, *Help them to see*. She told her father she'd confided this to Sister Helen, who said it meant there was much work to be done.

Jhana-Merise told her father of another dream she had. It was of the terrorist, Abd al Hashim. He was teaching her about the signs in a butterfly's wings.

Vincente was unnerved by this.

"My life is not my own anymore, Father. Unseen hands are guiding me. You know that. You've known that a long time."

His body vibrated with a new dread.

She told him she not only had dreamt of Hashim, but also of a young boy, and that they would be part of a group to help unlock a code within a sacred tablet in the desert. A tablet buried a long time ago, waiting to be awakened.

Vincente trembled at the thought of a mystery so huge and dangerous. A mystery with which his daughter seemed to be on intimate terms.

Jhana-Merise explained the providence of Arama leading them here, and of Sister Helen's connection to them—the convent a way-station on their way to America.

"America?" Vincente said, confused and alarmed. "How can we go to America?"

"Sister Helen will provide all that we need. She's helped us before. We've been here before. You and mother taught me that. It's what you said to her when you first met."

He remembered joking upon meeting his future wife for the first time that the reason they were so connected was they must've known each other in a previous life. It was forward of him to say such a thing in a culture steeped in an insular dogma. And that his future wife hadn't laughed, at what he thought was a brazen attempt at romance, struck him at a deep level of the possible truth in what he'd said, or at least that she believed it. And because he was falling in love with her, he believed it, too.

In the early days of their marriage Vincente and his wife had studied the history of past lives, even coming to believe the supposition with which he first flirted with her. And, after her death, he'd placed even more faith in its tenants, wanting, needing it to be real in order that he might see her again.

And now, with his daughter waiting for him to accept what she believed lie ahead, he could no longer deny that he, too, was being guided by the same unseen hands.

"What you seek will challenge all the precepts for which the religion we know has been based."

"Yes. It will challenge all those beliefs, Father.

PART FOUR

Surrender

42

Wednesday, September 23

It was sunrise, and the air was heavy with an early-approaching fall. Parked behind the fence of the neighborhood playground across the street from Dominique's apartment, Nazir and Taliq watched as the light in Dominique's bedroom clicked on.

It was an odd experience for Nazir, to observe life from a quiet family neighborhood and not the killing fields of his youth. He'd been thrown from the blood and heat of battle into a world of patience and surveillance, hoping Dominique would lead him to Hashim.

From their rented dark blue Nissan, Taliq watched a black sedan a half block down the street.

Nazir watched Dominique's silhouette go by the curtains as she passed, hurriedly, through the rooms.

Dominique rushed out of her apartment. A cab was waiting.

Nazir was about to pull out and follow. Taliq grabbed the wheel. "Wait," he said.

"Why?"

Taliq nodded in the direction of the black sedan.

"Someone else is watching her, too."

The black sedan pulled out and followed the cab.

"Go ahead, but not too close," Taliq said.

Nazir was annoyed at Taliq's officious attitude, but he'd seen the other car and Nazir hadn't. He followed both vehicles at a distance.

43

Dominique got out of the cab and made her way up the sidewalk to Senator Ledge's home. Julian watched from inside through an opening in the foyer curtains. Further up the street he saw the lights of the black government sedan go out.

He opened the front door. The entrance into the house was dark—its atmosphere of a mausoleum.

"What the hell is going on that you're being so mysterious about?"

He pulled her inside and shut the door.

"Hashim is gone. He left the cottage sometime in the last thirty-six hours and hasn't come back."

"I knew this was madness."

He pulled her into the den, seething.

"She has no fucking idea where he is?"

"No. She had work to do in D.C., and left him alone there."

"I knew it. I knew it. He played us! She can't 'see' where he is?"

"She's not a machine."

"Did you ask?"

"Yes."

"What'd she say?"

"She's not a machine."

"Jesus Christ. We're *fucked*."

Julian pulled the damask curtain aside and trained his eyes on the black government sedan, the interior dome light was on. They weren't trying to be invisible.

"They're going to follow us, you know, until they find out what we were hiding, or what we just fucking lost."

He wanted to break everything in the room. He picked up a paperweight from the desk and was about to hurl it into the wall.

Dominique grabbed his arm.

"That won't solve anything."

She took the paperweight from him.

"I don't believe he played us, Julian."

"Yeah. Well... We can't do this alone anymore. We've got to convince someone we're not insane."

Senator Ledge walked in.

"Oh. I'm sorry. I didn't know we had a guest. Good morning, Miss Valen."

"Good morning, Senator."

"I need some papers and I'll be on my way."

He went to the desk, opened a drawer, and collected a folder.

Ledge recoiled when Julian touched his hand. His face flushed when he realized it was a gesture of need, not aggression.

Julian looked to Dominique. They each knew what was about to come down.

"Are you sure?" she asked Julian.

Ledge was still, but not serene at the weight of her words.

"What is it?" he asked, his voice deep with concern.

Judgment and anger still hung there for Julian with his father. But they needed help. And if Ledge couldn't, or wouldn't help them, their lives were over—either way.

"We need to tell you what happened in the desert."

The senator's eyes fixed on his son. He was seeing a ghost. A ghost that would threaten more than the career the senator had been so desperate to save all those decades ago. And he knew this was what he'd longed for. Avoided. And feared. And with grave tenderness he said, "Tell me what happened."

44

The Virginia Beach boardwalk was deserted. The tumble of waves and the caw of seagulls haunted the air of the late September morning.

Hashim wasn't clear what path to take and without that certain mooring, his mind wandered as he paced the waterfront.

He'd imagined going to FBI Headquarters and surrendering. There were no lawyers involved when he imagined himself there. He would be alone.

The Prophet Muhammad had called the inner struggle for faith the Greater Jihad. This was the jihad of the soul. That all focus had been on what was called the Lesser Jihad, and the grief of all the tortures and deaths he'd orchestrated through that belief, filled Hashim with anguish.

He thought of all that annihilation and how he'd never been harmed. He knew he'd been in the CIA's sights a long time—they'd tracked him closer than bin Laden, but were never able to kill him. They'd stared at him from halfway across the globe with high-powered technology and missed. He'd been watched as he'd walked through mud-walled compounds, his life within their grasp, yet they'd always failed. Why?

A clear destiny descended.

That he'd shared a piece of his youth in that poem with Catherine, a stranger, was another sign of that destiny unfolding. He had not shared that with anyone in his life. He'd never been in love, except for the love he'd had for Allah and his people. He saw now that was an aberrant love, and he'd led sensitive young men to violent ends with that love, and the promise of an afterlife where dark-eyed virgins, chaste as pearls, waited.

And in the flood of remorse, he accepted his destiny. And knew it would end with the sacrifice of his life.

45

Senator Ledge entered Charles Bruton's office at the Pentagon. The room looked every bit as stately as the Oval Office. Plush blue carpet, shined oak desk, the American flag behind it.

The men shook hands.

"I'm glad Julian came home okay," Bruton said, a sorrow hung on him like lost faith.

"Me too," Ledge answered, a deep respect for that sorrow laced both words.

"How's Martha?" Bruton asked.

"She's fine."

Bruton moved to the oval table next to his desk and sat. He motioned for Ledge to do the same, but Ledge was too anxious to sit.

"Can I get you anything? Coffee?"

"No thanks."

Bruton leaned back in the chair and said, "So, what did you want to see me about?"

Off what Julian and Dominique had told him, Ledge had planned the strategy of how he might broach the subject of their contact with Hashim, but a photo of Bruton's son on the table caught him by surprise.

"The pain never goes away," Bruton said.

"I know. I'm sorry."

"You're one of the lucky ones. Your son came home alive. Is that what's bothering you? Guilt?"

"That never goes away, either."

"Peace comes hard. And harder in these days of trying to manage ourselves and the world."

Ledge looked at him, his eyes crushed in thought. He went back over the arc of their friendship, searching for clues as to how to proceed and what to reveal. He and Bruton had shared political secrets, but the repercussions of what he was holding now were grim at best.

Campaigning for his senate seat a fourth time, Ledge came back immediately when he'd found out that Bruton's son had come home in a body bag from a CIA mission in Afghanistan. That deepened their bond. But would that bond withstand what Julian and Dominique had told the senator of Hashim? He wouldn't know unless he took the chance.

"What if Hashim is here to surrender?"

Bruton stared at Ledge, chuckled and said, "Surrender? Where did you get that idea?"

Faced with the truth of why he was here, Ledge realized it had all happened fast and he wasn't prepared to go through with saying it out loud, but he wanted to plant a seed.

"You remember Jack Dean?"

"I try to forget ex-CIA who insist on chasing ghosts," Bruton answered. "Like the tablet he claimed was hidden in the desert over there. And you believed him enough at the time to have us go search for it."

"We were desperate to get any leverage we could against Saddam. But this isn't one of Dean's theories."

"Whose is it?"

Ledge stared at the photo of Bruton's son. It gave him time to think.

He'd been convinced of what Julian and Dominique told him was the truth about Hashim, yet being here, he wasn't ready for the barrage of questions and accusations Bruton would throw at him if he pursued it. He sidestepped the issue and sat down opposite Bruton.

"We were good friends once. I'm not sure what happened to that."

"Life has many turns. And you were the one responsible for pulling away. Is that why you're here? To mend the past?"

"Maybe I came to ask forgiveness."

"You don't need me to forgive you, Paul."

Ledge missed his friendship with Bruton. He was the one man he'd been able to talk with. But that closeness never gave way to him sharing with Bruton the fact he'd had experiences he couldn't explain—experiences that placed in his life a chance to move the axis of the world away from violence.

He was a young senator when his occurrence happened, placed into that position by forces outside the world he knew, to help the world of which he was a part. Fear had stopped him from taking that on, and created a void in his life—a void responsible for the growing dissolution in his marriage, and a void between he and his son.

Julian was being given the chance to make that right, and Ledge knew he wouldn't be able to escape his responsibility any longer.

He came wanting to come clean, and tell Bruton about his past, and what his son and Dominique told him of what happened to them in the desert, and that Hashim was here to surrender.

But what if Hashim came for something else?

The one thing of which he was aware—*Hashim was here*. The reason would surface sooner or later.

That unknown gripped the courage he wanted to have, and again kept him silent.

46

In front of the raw concrete monolithic structure on Pennsylvania Avenue, Hashim stood at the metal sign above the doors to the FBI that read: *J. Edgar Hoover Building.* A metallic taste was in his mouth. The bitterness of saliva upon his lips. But he was here. He had no idea if he would make a difference. And who would believe him? But he was compelled to be here.

He knew Julian and Dominique couldn't risk their lives to give witness. Any empathy they showed would condemn them. He knew he'd be in this alone. He'd come to that realization soon after their lives were spared in the attack in the Mosul desert. His journey to America had fueled his resolve that something this radical and expiatory was needed, in order to shift the unending violence. He also knew the blood and turmoil a surrender of this magnitude could create. But it was what had been placed before him, and he chose the path that led him here—and he stepped inside the front doors of the FBI.

He held up his hands, told the guards who he was, and went down to his knees.

Next thing he knew agents surrounded him.

The barrels of six Glocks pointed at his head.

47

Hashim's hands and feet were shackled, and his wrists chained to an unmovable metal desk. He was in a room in the pallid basement of the Hoover building. Across the room, a camera was directed toward him, its red light on.

There were voices on the other side of the door. The door handle moved, then stopped, as if the person on the other side were thinking before entering.

The door opened.

The energy in the room shifted as Adrien Kurt walked in.

"We'll be right outside, Doctor Kurt," one of the two armed military men said when they closed the door.

Hashim stared at Kurt. There was something familiar about him.

"I trust you were read your Miranda Rights," Kurt said, as he sat across from Hashim.

"Yes," Hashim answered.

"So, you understand that everything you say can and will be used against you?"

"Yes."

"And that everything you say here is being recorded?"

"I understand."

"Good. My name is Adrien Kurt. I'm a psychiatrist and here to determine whether or not you're of sound mind."

"I understand."

Kurt leaned back in the metal chair. It scraped against the concrete floor.

The two men studied each other. In spite of Kurt's grim pose, Hashim saw a warmth in the eyes of the man across from him.

"How did you get to America?" Kurt asked.

"We have many ways to get what we need. Much like how your intelligence gets what it needs."

"And, you're willing to give us that information?"

"Yes."

"Who knows you're here?"

"I would think everyone by now."

"Not everyone. Who knew you were leaving Mosul?"

"No one. It was my decision alone."

"But you got a passport as 'Nicolas Sandor.'"

"Those who provided me with it did not know its purpose."

"So, no one knows why you came here?"

"Correct."

"So, why are you here? And what's the purpose of your surrender? If indeed that's what it is."

Hashim's nose was running and he tried to wipe it, but his hands couldn't reach his face chained to the metal table.

Kurt took out a small packet of tissues from his jacket pocket. He removed one, and wiped Hashim's nose for him.

He folded the tissue inside a clean one and tossed it into the trashcan against the wall.

"Thank you."

This was a far cry from the way Hashim's interrogations had gone. He'd studied the Inquisition of the Middle Ages, the judicial system of the Roman Catholic Church, whose aim was to combat heresy, and the techniques of torture the U.S. military had perfected in their black sites. Hashim learned much from his fellow men.

"I'll ask again. What is your purpose here?"

Hashim looked down at the chains on his wrists.

"I discovered things about myself under bin Laden. I learned I was violent, brutal, and determined. I'd beheaded enemies, and ordered them to be killed. But I was misguided."

"How have you come to this now?"

He wanted to tell Kurt it was the experience in the desert that led him here. How the visions of who he'd been in the swirl of dust and light erased the darkness that had saturated him with hate. Somehow, he knew Kurt would understand. But those who were privy to this conversation, from wherever they watched and listened, he wouldn't trust with this truth. But he needed to let Kurt know somehow, and words from the Qur'an ran through his mind, and he spoke them.

"'I tell you of a truth that the spirits which now have affinity shall be kindred together although they all meet in new persons and names.'"

And Kurt said, "'Every soul will be brought face to face with the good that it has done and with the evil it has done.'"

"You know the Qur'an."

"Yes. Very well."

The psychiatrist's eyes were locked in on the prisoner.

A breath rushed out of Hashim, like he was expelling his past, and he said, "In Islam there are two types of jihad."

"I know. The greater, of the soul. And the lesser, of the sword."

"I'm here to show the world the greater, and that our violent jihad is wrong."

Kurt leaned in, his elbows on the table inches from Hashim's hands. "And how do you expect to show the world that?"

"In a courtroom, with all the coverage your country is known for."

"And you expect to have a legal team help you do that?"

"There is no defense for what I've done."

"It's hard to believe your motive is to offer yourself up with nothing in return. You could use this platform for your lesser jihad."

"How you deal with me is up to you. I am in your hands. This is neither simple nor easy, nor will be, for either of us. But I am here."

He took another deep breath—this time the air that rushed out had the scent of roses. He could see Kurt's breathing changed as well. And from the look in Kurt's eyes, and his slow intake of breath, Hashim could tell he smelled the roses, too.

48

The White House was in a frenzy. There was no precedent for a terrorist's surrender. Was it a tactical distraction away from an imminent attack? What ploy was behind Hashim's surrender? How could this be contained for maximum security and played for political cachet?

This was a long-awaited moment, but the way it occurred opened a Pandora's box the government hadn't expected. Where the trial would be held was also a serious matter. All the options had risk: Federal Court. International Tribunal. Military Court. Foreign Court. U.N. National Court. U.N. Administered Court in Afghanistan. Or a Special Islamic Court. And so, the White House was in a frenzy.

The heads of the FBI and Justice Department gathered at the Pentagon to review all the evidence, testimony, and details they had regarding the criminal and his crimes. Someone played Hashim's last video warning, which came right before the feed from the warehouse. The bearded face of the cleric peered out from the monitor—anger burned thick in his eyes.

"What America has experienced is but a fraction of what my people have endured," Hashim seethed. "Our sons have been slain, blood has been shed, and our sacred places defiled. Millions of children have been killed in Iraq though they were guilty of nothing. Yet no one has condemned this. You are hypocrites, and the events you have perpetuated have divided the world. To the people of America I say, you will not be safe until your armies quit the land of Muhammad. Until that day, worse than towers falling will you forever see from the wrath of Allah on your people."

Bin Laden had taught him well.

This was one of many pieces of evidence the prosecution planned to use in building its case against the cleric. But there were concerns. While the United States led the world in prosecuting terrorists, the burden of proof was high as to the crimes with which they could connect him in a federal court. It would hinder efforts to bring Hashim to justice no matter how much evidence they'd collected. The prosecutors might be unwilling to use sensitive information that was derived from top-secret sources. The location of the trial and prison where Hashim could be held would become a magnet for violence. No matter where he was detained and prosecuted, firestorms would ignite. Now, they had to figure into the equation the fact Hashim had surrendered. Whatever the American government and its lawyers didn't know about Hashim could be used against them. Capturing and arresting a terrorist was one thing, surrender this phenomenal another. The government could be guaranteed Hashim's people would reach him when they discovered what he'd done if they already hadn't. They would question his loyalty, and put a fatwa on him to be sure. This added enormous complexity and strain to an already insurmountable task.

49

Friday, September 25

From his window seat on the plane, Vincente looked at his gruff image reflected back in the small oval glass as he took in the warmth and beauty of the morning sun.

He, Jhana-Merise, and Arama had been flying all night from Peru. That Sister Helen had furnished them with passports and him a work visa brought a smile to his face, and deeper respect for the maverick she was. It even helped him look at the man on the cross with renewed interest—that he could inspire such action in the cause of a young girl's destiny. Truth was, that man had inspired a religion, so why not passports and a work visa.

In the time Jhana-Merise spent at the convent, Vincente read about cuneiforms and codes in sacred texts. The scrutiny, science, and passion he discovered in those who'd explored these things seemed to be grounded in plausible reality. Like the idea of past lives his wife, and now Jhana-Merise, had exposed him to. And so, he presented what he'd found to Helen a few days before he got on the plane. He believed she would be open to the discussion. He was right.

Helen wasn't surprised Jhana-Merise had said there was a hidden tablet in the desert. After all, Helen had said, *Moses was in possession of two tablets, who's to say there weren't others yet to be discovered?*

Vincente closed his eyes, picturing Helen's sweet face, and thought of the last thing this holy woman had said to him before he left with his daughter.

The wolf will live with the lamb, the leopard will lie down with the young goat. The calf and the lion will graze together. And a little child shall lead them.

The faith he'd called a "useless devotion" upon his wife's death took on a different light in those meetings with Sister Helen. There was a world beyond the one he'd been preached to about. A world this nun had deep interest and curiosity in as well. A world that held, as possible, the belief that we are more than we know, and there are many willing to risk their lives for it.

Jhana-Merise leaned her head against her father's side, opened her eyes and smiled, as if she'd heard what he'd been thinking.

He kissed her gently on her forehead.

She reached out to Arama sitting in the aisle seat.

The plane's wheels hit the ground with a thud. They'd landed at Dulles.

Vincente gazed at his daughter. She was a delicate and powerful being. He looked at his own rough-hewn hands and still felt much the brute. But within the gap of those opposites he knew something was reaching to be born.

50

Arama stood at the door to Isabel's apartment. She'd not warned her sister she was coming. And while her unexpected arrival would make Isabel furious, that she brought two others would test their already fragile relationship. But Arama believed once she reminded her sister of the importance of their mission she would understand.

The apartment door opened and Arama saw in her sister's eyes the anger she expected, but it was now dressed in the latest style. A dark blue suit of impeccable taste and expense, like so many American women wore on TV.

Arama gazed into the apartment. It lacked warmth and light, from the straight lines of the furniture, to the hardwood floor, and venetian blinds shut so tight that light had to squeeze into the room. And there was a fragrance she'd never smelled before. It must've come from a bottle, not nature, she thought.

"What the hell are you doing here?" Isabel said, jarred at the sudden presence of her sister.

"May we come in?" Arama asked, pointing to the two others, as if there was nothing bizarre in this sudden appearance in her sister's life after so long a time.

"This is the young girl I left you the message about who cured the boy. Her name is Jhana-Merise. And this is her father, Vincente. They're friends of mine."

Arama saw Isabel's body stiffen and her jaw clench. She used to be afraid of her sister's anger, but standing here at the threshold of her sister's life, and looking into the apartment with its cold modernity, she felt pride in how she'd chosen to live. She was a worker from a poor land, but that land bred dreams of family and unity, not the arid dreams of greed and separateness she saw her sister had fallen into.

"You can't show up like this," Isabel said in an angry whisper, her hands clenched by her side.

The distance had allowed Arama to deny the extent of rage to which her sister was capable. Yes, they had walked different paths. They'd walked them for decades, but Arama hoped that something this magnificent could break through Isabel's emotional wall. They weren't from two separate countries, they were human beings connected by God, no matter how much Isabel needed possessions to prove her worth.

Arama told Isabel of Jhana-Merise and how she healed the boy. She also told her of dreams Jhana-Merise had of Hashim teaching her about the butterfly, and how she saw him clean-shaven, with hands and feet chained. Arama could see her unexpected presence and all the information she'd blurted had her sister reeling. She also saw Isabel take a deep breath, collect herself, as she always had in her drive to be superior, and in true lawyer fashion cross-examine the young girl she just met.

"You've seen Hashim in dreams?" Isabel said, her facade masked the alarm running through her.

"Yes," Jhana-Merise replied.

"Who else knows of this?"

"Don't worry. God will protect us," Arama answered.

"This is serious," Isabel said to Arama, pointing a finger like a gun. "Have you told anyone else about these dreams, Jhana-Merise?"

"Only a nun in a convent where we stayed before coming here."

"And Sister Helen is on our side," Arama said.

Vincente watched the whole exchange, his face flushed with embarrassment.

"This isn't what you expected. I'm sorry," Vincente said, and turned to go, but his daughter didn't move.

"Jhana-Merise," Vincente ordered her to follow him, but again, she didn't move.

Father and daughter stood on the landing.

Arama stayed just outside the apartment door.

Isabel just inside, protecting her kingdom.

The map of Isabel's life was intricate. It had taken her from South America to Washington, but it was a more tortuous route than it seemed on the surface.

Living and working in D.C. was something she'd wished for, growing up in a third world country in the shadow of America. And she broke free from the primitive land of the Incas and worked her way to becoming a U.S. citizen. She'd put herself through school in D.C., then university, then law school, working three part-time jobs: clerk, receptionist, and maid. By day she'd been an ambitious student competing for the most coveted law positions, by night, an invisible service worker dismissed as someone from a country far below the United States.

Her ambitions came from her mother, and when she died, Isabel's passion to leave the land of her birth overwhelmed her and there was no turning back. Isabel knew Arama had a passion too—for magical thinking and omens. Something Isabel believed was foolish. But it now played havoc in her mind. For as much as she wanted them gone, what clairvoyant ability this young girl—whom her sister had placed before her—seemed to have, Isabel needed to know the full measure of.

If this young girl had dreams of Hashim, of what else was she capable that would need to be contained?

Isabel stepped aside and offered them a place to stay for the night. She didn't know Arama had plans for them to be here longer.

51

The occurrence in the desert, and the miracle of her survival added to Dominique's cachet. But it was her literary street cred and a call from Bruton that opened the door to the Department of Justice.

The White House was more than eager to set her up with access to the pending trial they'd been preparing since they'd known Hashim was on American soil. They couldn't avoid media scrutiny, and thought the best way would be to make the first move and get out in front of the story before it broke. And they believed Dominique was the ideal journalist to help them disseminate that information, before all hell broke loose, and every media outlet clamored for coverage.

Through the series of meetings they let her sit in on, Dominique was brought up to speed with their plan for prosecuting Hashim in D.C. It needed to happen fast, because the longer they waited the more time the insurgents had to plan freeing or killing him.

Dominique had gathered background information on all the principle lawyers. She was drawn to one in particular—the lone female lawyer on the case who'd come from very interesting circumstances. She asked if she might have time to discuss what she'd been working on with that lawyer. Dominique knew that lawyer's perspective would be unique among the others the Department of Justice had gathered.

52

Despite the demands of the case and the terrifying reality that had intruded into her life, Isabel Chavez was flattered by Dominique's interest in her part of the prosecution.

Isabel welcomed Dominique into her office in the criminal division of the Department of Justice. There were no windows, just a metal desk, two folding chairs and a massive set of filing cabinets that lined the prison-gray walls.

"It's a storage room, but we need all the space we can create," Isabel said, and motioned for Dominique to sit opposite her.

"Must be exciting, being part of the prosecution."

"It is."

"So, how's it going?"

It was a simple question and Dominique's smile was disarming.

"There's a lot to do."

"Have you been to see Hashim, yet?" Dominique asked.

"No. Few have that permission right now. Why do you think he surrendered?"

"The drone wasn't meant for the warehouse. Did you know that?" Dominique asked. She could see the piece of information shocked Isabel. "They didn't tell you."

"We were told there were extraordinary circumstances, but not what they were."

"Business as usual for the FBI."

"How might those circumstances affect our case against him?"

Dominique hesitated. There was method in her every word and every silence.

"I understand if you'd rather not answer that, Miss Valen."

"No. It's all right."

"Do you think those circumstances are responsible for his surrender?"

"You're the first person who's asked me that. Why do you think he surrendered?"

"We're not sure. There's been no activity from the cells since he walked into the FBI. We're not clear how to read that."

"What do you think?"

Isabel stared into the air. Dominique respected her hesitation. She knew there were too many unanswered questions for Isabel to make a conjecture that wasn't grounded in reality.

"I think there are two possibilities," Isabel said. "Either he's here to take down something huge…"

"You mean the White House."

"That's an educated guess. And maybe the cells are quiet for that reason. Or, he's here for something we don't yet understand."

"A lawyer who admits there's something they don't understand. I'm impressed."

She asked what she believed was an innocent question. "You have a sister in Cuzco?"

Dominique saw Isabel's body tense, and she sat up in her chair as if she'd been called on by a teacher for not paying attention.

"My sister has nothing to do with what we're talking about. Why bring her into this?"

It was a defensive reply and piqued Dominique's curiosity.

"Finding things about people is what I do. It gives me a better picture."

"My sister and I haven't talked to each other in a long time."

Dominique could feel Isabel wanted to take the conversation away from her sister, but Dominique didn't let her.

"Then you're not aware there was a supposed miracle at the hospital where she works."

"Really?" Isabel said, feigning innocence.

Her response left Dominique with the sense there was more here than met the eye.

"I spent time in Peru before the Middle East. Hiked Machu Picchu. Spent a couple of weeks in Cuzco. Made some friends. They're still there. They have some interesting beliefs."

"I come from a culture that takes little responsibility for itself, Miss Valen. God will make all things better. They never look at what their part is in circumstances."

Isabel was digging herself deeper into Dominique's curiosity.

"That's not always true," Dominique said, working the conversation.

"Does this have something to do with what happened in the warehouse?"

Isabel was desperate to shift the attention off her sister and the miracle.

"I guess I'm like some of those in your culture. I believe in miracles. That I'm alive is testament to that."

"Would Hashim consider it a miracle? Him being alive?"

Isabel queried like a lawyer desperate to change the subject.

Dominique smiled at Isabel's attempt to turn the discussion around.

"Ask him when you get him in court," Dominique said, knowing there was something she'd touched on that Isabel was evading. Dominique would find out what that was.

53

From their Nissan, parked across the street from the Department of Justice, Nazir and Taliq waited. They'd been following Dominique for days. It was late afternoon. A raging thunderstorm had the people on the street running for cover. Taliq's burner phone chirped with a text. He looked down at the message.

"Is that from Sarif?" Nazir asked.

"Yeah," Taliq said, lying.

"What did he say?"

"Same old, same old. 'Where's Hashim?'"

But it wasn't from Sarif. It was from Taliq's contact at the FBI. It said: Getting hot. Get out!

Taliq knew as soon as the cells found out about Hashim there would be orders to assassinate him, so Taliq needed to extricate himself before the shitstorm hit, and he'd be in the crossfire. But there were things he still wanted to know.

"I'm gonna ask you for the last time. What happened in the warehouse?"

Nazir glared at him.

"I'm not the enemy, Nazir. You've got to lighten up."

Nazir grabbed the burner phone from Taliq's twitchy hand.

Taliq tried to wrench it back but Nazir pulled out a switchblade and flicked it open.

"Whoa, whoa. Take it easy. You need to lighten up. It's a fucking phone. Give it back."

Taliq grabbed for the phone but Nazir swiped the blade across Taliq's knuckles.

"Whoa. Jesus. What the fuck. You crazy?"

Nazir flipped open the lid of the burner and read the text.

Taliq leaned forward and reached his hand around to his back.

"This isn't from Sarif."

"You're too fucking paranoid. Sarif's not the only game in town. You don't know all the players."

"Who are the players? Tell me."

"Put the knife away, okay? We're civilized men."

Taliq pulled out the Glock from the back of his belt.

Nazir made a split-second decision.

A flash of metal.

Taliq's eyes widened with the realization his throat had been cut. All the years of preparation to infiltrate the cell. The estrangement from all he'd known, ending. He thought the road out would be torturous. Prolonged interrogation if caught. He'd always feared he'd give up secrets when the pain became unbearable. He gasped for what air he could. But it didn't help. He slumped down in the passenger seat. His head hit the window with a thud. He was dead.

None but a few at the FBI knew Taliq was undercover and they would never let that information out. Taliq was collateral damage.

Nazir panicked. He turned on the ignition, peeled out, and just as quick jammed his brakes when he saw Dominique crossing the road, looking at him.

The car slid sideways on the slick road and stopped right in front of her.

Nazir stared at Dominique.

She stood, defiant, daring him to move.

The last time they were this close was when they'd almost died in the desert.

The rain pounded.

The car idled as he waited to see what she would do.

She approached the driver's side door and looked at him through the closed window.

She saw the inert body in the passenger seat.

"This is either a strange coincidence, or you've been following me," she said to him through the glass. "And from the looks of it, your friend is dead, and you're in a predicament you're not sure how to get out of."

"He's not my friend," Nazir said through the glass.

"Then, I imagine you could use some help."

54

A group has a nervous system. It has a heart and a soul that experiences the same love and fear. Dominique was at the center of this force. What the Ancient Greeks called, Pneuma. *That which is breathed.*

It was this collective breath that put her here at this specific place and time and allowed her to get into the backseat of the car.

In the weeks she'd been back, Dominique had found out more about cuneiforms.

The Sumerian stones were indeed the oldest written records on the planet. Fifty-eight hundred years old. But they described things that happened billions of years earlier than that, and in great detail.

The ancient Sumerians were telling us a story of history that's difficult to accept because of our certainty that what we know about the past is all there is to know.

She read the controversial works of Zecharia Sitchin. He wrote about many cities that were described in the Bible: Babylon, Akkad, and Erech, which for a long time people thought were myths because no one could prove their existence. There wasn't even the slightest sign they'd existed. Then archaeologists found one city, which led to another, and another, eventually finding all of the cities mentioned in the Bible. These excavators and explorers of the past dug into the layers of these ancient ruins and discovered thousands of clay tablets on which the history of Sumer, and the history of the Earth were recorded in great detail, going back eons.

The echo of remembrance reverberated through Dominique, and she knew without knowing that those she was now connected to were part of a nervous system, and she was at the center of that which is breathed.

She dialed a number on her mobile.

"What are you doing?" Nazir demanded, watching her in the rearview.

"I'm calling someone to help us," she said, as she looked at the dead body of Taliq in the front passenger seat—his neck still draining blood.

55

Dominique and Nazir stood in the kitchen of Catherine's Virginia Beach cottage. It was more lived in since Hashim had spent time here. Covers had been removed from the furniture. Pots were on the stove. The kitchen table was set, looking like company was expected.

Dominique stared at the text on Taliq's burner. *Getting hot. Get out!*

"Who was he?" Nazir asked.

"Julian's finding out."

"He had no identification?"

"No."

"And his body?"

"I'm not sure what Julian is doing with that."

She looked at Nazir bent over the kitchen sink, head in his hands.

"Did you plan to kill him?"

"No. But I never trusted him."

She remembered first setting eyes on Nazir in the warehouse and thinking if jihad was attracting young men this sensitive and strong there was more to fear than anyone could imagine. Now, here he was, this young man. Frightened. Isolated from the world he knew. Alone.

Nazir reminded her of her brother when they were younger, with all the promise and apprehension of youth. She saw that promise and apprehension before her. And an inextricable bond. Something relentless had brought them together. And she knew they were on their own to find out what.

"How old were you when your parents were killed?"

Nazir turned to her, his eyes spheres of sorrow, as if she was looking into his heart.

She saw his sorrow ease when she got that he knew she cared.

"Hashim told me they'd died in an attack."

Nazir's breathing calmed and he said, "I was six."

"You've been fighting ever since?"

"Yes."

Dominique remembered what Catherine told her about what Hashim had written when he was boy.

> *There are stories we carry inside that have slipped beyond the veil of consciousness and wait until a certain time. And, as a falcon descends upon its prey, we rise up more fierce and hungry than the falcon, through ashes at the merest fraction of light, grasping, trembling for God.*

She saw that trembling in the young man before her.

"What happened to you in the warehouse?" she asked.

Nazir's eyes took in the pale light of the moon as it brushed through the kitchen.

He looked at her.

She could see he was lost. She knew that he, too, was leaving the stories—ones he'd believed all his life—behind. Stories dissolving like the sunlight after the bomb hit the warehouse, as if it had been vacuumed into the air.

"I heard a voice," he said. "I'd never heard voices before."

"What did it say?"

His body tensed. She could see he wanted to avoid the answer.

"We all had something happen to us in the warehouse, Nazir. We're connected in a way we weren't before. What did the voice say to you?"

She remembered the first time she heard a voice in that hospital room in Pittsburgh, and how she dared not tell anyone. She reached for his hand. He moved away.

Julian entered the kitchen.

"What did you do with the body?" Nazir asked, rushing to him.

"What I needed to. But once the cells discover he's missing you'll be their prime suspect and wanted by your own people as well as the FBI."

"They're not my people." The words slipped out of Nazir's mouth. He turned away. Ashamed.

The hush gave way to the scent of roses.

Nazir turned back to them.

Dominique saw that what still held Julian rigid in doubt, and the fear and bewilderment that had kept Nazir in need of his past, were melting. And, in the opening of their hearts, Nazir said, "'Ask the lawyer about the girl.' That's what the voice said to me in the desert."

"What the hell does that mean?" Julian asked.

"It means we're on the right path," Dominique answered.

And she knew the relentless energy that had brought them together had weaved yet another thread deeper into their lives.

56

Saturday, September 26

In the dark hours before dawn, Hashim was brought out of his cell at FBI headquarters. He was dressed in civilian clothes and his hands and feet were shackled. He stepped into a Humvee and was positioned between two armed soldiers and across from three armed federal agents. There were two other follow vehicles. Two of the agents in the Humvee were young and on edge, their legs bounced. The third was older and Middle Eastern. He stared at Hashim. Hashim looked away, knowing the hatred he saw in the man's eyes didn't need the fuel of an imprisoned terrorist's gaze. Hashim heard the man's name when the men were talking. His name was Kareef.

When the convoy reached I-95, vehicles split off in different directions. The Humvee and two unmarked FBI cars took Route 1 North. Hashim was on his way to prison, trial, and likely death.

He watched the young men across and next to him. He noticed their fingers were white, knuckle-gripped around their weapons. This threw him back to his own fear—to the time he was a boy and his father had dropped him, from the boat they were in, into deep ocean water with one instruction: "Swim back if you want to live."

Hashim did swim back and saw his mother filled with relief and panic when he'd reached shore. It was here his mind had crystallized with the thought that nothing and no one was safe. Only rage assured survival.

Rage was the way to let the world know of the plight of his people. He believed bin Laden had come from that place, too, in the beginning. Diplomacy achieved nothing. Attention must be paid. Bombs led the way. They were an answer to ripping the cloak of invisibility from his world, and for the greater world to see the poverty and devastation that had befallen his people, in a land most had ignored. But the experience in the desert changed that. It changed him. Allah had spoken through the dust and destruction and metallic screech of the drone with these two words etched in the air: *Nahn wahid. We are One*. So simple, yet dismissed as unreal and unachievable. Life obliterated what God had designed.

But Hashim had been drilled down into the inexorable truth of his soul—that great transformation required greater sacrifice, not destruction. He knew the others who'd been with him now had the chance to harness the same truth.

After traveling six hours, Hashim saw the road sign: *Attica Correctional Facility*. He knew of the riots there in 1971. It was one of the bloodiest prison confrontations in American history. Thirteen hundred prisoners had rebelled, taken over the prison, and held forty guards hostage. They'd issued a list of demands, which included calls for improvements in living conditions as well as educational and training opportunities.

They'd even entered into negotiations with state officials, but negotiations failed and state police and National Guard troops seized the prison. Forty-three individuals, including ten hostages, were killed. It was believed a group of Black Muslims were responsible for the uprising. But the Black Muslims were exonerated when it was revealed they'd succeeded in preventing any revenge attacks against the unpopular corrections officers who'd been contained in what they called the "hostage circle." They also made them as comfortable as they could under the circumstances. They gave clothing to all the hostages who'd been stripped.

The occurrence at Attica was legend.

The convoy approached the Lock Gates of Attica. The vehicles stopped in front of the huge, thick black metal doors. The agents and National Guardsmen jumped out of the cars and swirled around Hashim as he got out of the Humvee.

Hashim entered inside Attica's walls via an exterior concrete catwalk.

Bars of cold steel greeted them as the soldiers and guards led Hashim through the internal hall of C Block.

The chains around his feet grated along pockmarked concrete. Bleak thoughts of his father, and the sweet but passive voice of his mother arose as if from the grave. He had been stripped of: stature, power, invincibility, and hope. What took its place was something he'd always dismissed as weakness. Something he now realized was all there was to embrace—the crumbling of hate.

57

The small Attica prison visiting room they met in had a chill that seeped from the mortar of its grim stone walls. Hashim was here with two lawyers assigned to defend him. They'd been here a few hours awaiting his arrival. The government wasn't wasting time. They sat in cheap chairs across a much-abused table—Hashim on one side, the duo on the other.

"Your surrender could work in our favor," said the man with a smoker's voice. His name was Carl Robinson.

"First thing we're asking for are pretrial discovery materials," the other lawyer, Terrence Keyser, said. He was younger than Robinson, with much more curiosity. "That's not going to make the prosecution happy, to have to hand over that kind of sensitive information, but it's the law."

The men talked of how they figured the prosecution would come at them and how they planned to defend Hashim.

"I have nothing to defend," Hashim said.

"This is America. We have what we call, 'The Rule of Law,'" Keyser told him.

"I know what that is. But I will speak for myself."

The two men looked at each other. Hashim could see they were confused.

Robinson cleared his throat.

"This is our job, whether we want to be here or not. We're trying to keep you from a death sentence."

"There's already a fatwa on me."

"We can't protect you from that. But we might be able to keep you from getting a lethal injection," Keyser said.

"I'm not afraid to die."

"Well, I guess we're wasting everyone's time here," Robinson said, annoyed, as he gathered his materials and placed them in his briefcase.

"Let me ask you something," Robinson said, as he stopped what he was doing. "Why did you agree to see us if you want to defend yourself?"

Hashim looked at them. They were a trial run. He didn't need them to represent him. He needed them to gauge their reactions to what he had to say. They represented the world he would be thrust into. A world of juries and judges.

"What I did was evil. Every action. Every order was designed for one purpose. To bring America, to bring the world, to its knees. And while I believe now that our jihad was wrong, and am willing to pay with my life for my actions, America is no less culpable in horrors. You've convinced yourselves you must police the world. In that is an inherent arrogance, and you've made as many enemies as you believe you have friends."

"You're not a hero, Hashim," Robinson said. "You're a wanted man. And you're lucky if you don't get a death sentence. So, don't tell me what's wrong with America. They're going to ask you to name names, name places, sites of coming attacks. And they will want all of the dummy companies that have been set up to filter the funds used for your jihad. You do that, then maybe…maybe you have a chance to convince any of us your words are something other than total bullshit."

"I understand," Hashim said. "Might you be able to arrange the transaction of this information to happen in private?"

"You don't want to go to trial now? Is that what you're telling us?" Keyser said.

"I did want that platform. But it was arrogant of me to think it would have any other purpose than to create turmoil that would serve no one."

"We'll take your request to our superiors. Is there anything else you want to say?"

"No." Hashim said as he stood up. His eyes didn't waver from theirs.

"Thank you for doing whatever you can."

Robinson picked up his briefcase and moved out.

Keyser lingered.

Hashim could see he was trying to figure him out.

"You coming?" Robinson called, before the guard opened the door for him to leave.

"Give me a minute," Keyser answered.

"I'll be in the car. Don't take all day," Robinson said, and walked out.

Keyser and Hashim were alone.

"What's your deal?" Keyser asked.

"I don't know that you would understand."

"Try me."

In his car in the Attica parking lot, Robinson was on the phone with the Attorney General. He told him of Hashim's change of mind, to not be brought into a court.

The secret hope the government had was that the jihadi leader would never be captured alive, making a trial unnecessary—but they had to deal with reality. They discussed that while some of the prosecutors believed the image of Hashim sitting, chained, in a courtroom would be an eye-opening visual for those who thought he was invincible, there were others who were conflicted at the extraordinary difficulties posed by this scenario, and maintained there would be no way to provide adequate security. More important, it would be near impossible to select an unbiased jury. And there were those who thought it would send a horrible message to the world to not hold a trial because of those threats.

"The hell with what he wants," the Attorney General said on the other end of the mobile. "He's going to trial."

Keyser came out of the prison and made his way to the car. He got in the passenger side and shut the door.

Robinson looked at him. He could see Keyser was shaken.

"What the fuck happened?" Robinson asked.

"I'm not sure."

"That's no answer. What did he say?"

"Forget it. It's crazy."

"We're not moving until you tell me. Or I'll go back in there and find out. I'm not playing games."

Keyser was uncomfortable with what he was being forced to say.

"You can tell me, or the Attorney General."

He turned on the ignition.

Keyser turned it off.

"He told me what happened in the warehouse."

"What did he say?"

"You won't believe it."

"Try me."

Keyser told him about the swirling light and the butterfly and the sound.

Robinson howled.

"Did you just make that shit up?"

The look on Keyser's face was dead serious.

"He's fucking with you, man. And you're crazy if you think anyone is going to believe it. And you're nuts if you do."

PART FIVE

The Tablets

58

Sunday, September 27

Senator Ledge never thought he'd contact Jack Dean again. Decades earlier, Dean had claimed to have information relating to an object he said the government called, "The Tablet." Dean had top security clearance at the time. But after it had been discovered he was about to reveal to a larger audience what he knew...he was discredited and dismissed from service.

The senator knew of a similar scenario around that same time. A number of other governments were involved in the study of various aspects of the paranormal. The mission: to evaluate through reverse engineering how vulnerable to psychic spying U.S. intelligence agencies and their secrets were. This was done to such a degree of accuracy that Department of Defense and Army officials decided to change the emphasis from assessing vulnerabilities to collecting intelligence information via the paranormal against America's Cold War adversaries. The senator also knew that years after that, before the first book written by a psychic spy was about to go to print, this secret Department of Defense program got cancelled and the book debunked before its release. The senator knew why. He knew the media attention had the potential to blow the lid off government secrets regarding its history of paranormal inquiries.

Dean and Ledge had been friends. But as soon as all that came down, Ledge got as far away as he could from his reputation being tainted. Career trumped friendship. But ever since Julian's return, Jack Dean hadn't been far from Ledge's mind.

Ledge made his way up the stone steps to Dean's red brick, Baltimore City Row Home, and rang the bell.

Dean answered the door, a cane in hand. He looked older than Ledge remembered. But the tweed jacket on his broad shoulders, Ledge didn't forget.

"You've aged much better than I," Dean said, full voiced and pompous. He'd always spoken loud and with authority. "Come on in, Paul."

Ledge followed Dean into the living room.

"How's Emily?" Ledge asked.

"She's in Milan for a trade show."

"She's still doing well. Good for her."

"Me too. She saved me when I tried to take my life all those years ago. Isn't that what your children are supposed to do? What friends are supposed to do?"

The accusation made Ledge bristle.

"But let that be water under our burnt bridge," Dean added.

"If you want me to leave, Jack…"

"Don't be an ass."

He struggled to sit on the sofa.

Ledge moved to help.

Dean waved him off.

Ledge sat down and smiled.

"Missed me, huh?" Dean said.

"You have a way of never going away, Jack."

"Yep. A way that's assured my isolation. I could be the King of Molokai."

"What?"

"It's where they toss the lepers."

He adjusted on the sofa with difficulty.

"Fucking arthritis."

He took in a deep breath and let out a low growl. "So…"

Dean folded his arms and waited.

Ledge hesitated, unsure how to begin.

"Why don't you tell me what you know, Paul. Or, do you think I'd think you're crazy?"

"I don't know you'd ever think anyone was crazy, Jack."

"I'll take that as a compliment. We've got bad blood between us. So what? You wouldn't be here unless you needed my help. Consider yourself lucky I'm alive."

Ledge stared at the man he had called friend, ashamed he'd abandoned him all those years ago.

"Your son and the journalist found something in the warehouse, didn't they?"

"They found a couple of things."

Dean rested both hands atop his cane. He did look like a king.

"It's a force that won't be stopped. Something happened after the drone made its mysterious reversal to the warehouse. That's what brought Hashim here."

Ledge was shocked Dean could know this top-secret information.

"I didn't burn all my bridges. Tell me what you know."

"You seem to know what I know."

"Not bad for an old guy who's been banished from your world, huh? Okay. Do with this what you will."

Ledge watched Dean settle into his professorial mode.

"It's believed that carved into the tablet are instructions from ancient Sumerians whose civilization began almost overnight in 3800

BC. This is what you ran away from all those years ago. Their code has been unbreakable because it's supposed to lead to a portal that opens to a higher consciousness. A consciousness humans aren't ready to possess."

"And, how do you know this, Jack?"

"Because I didn't panic. Now, let's start with cuneiforms."

Ledge studied this brave, solitary ancient in a tweed jacket.

"Cuneiforms aren't all that rare. Many have been found but never translated until a Sumerian scholar—"

"Zecharia Sitchin," Ledge interjected. They were nothing if not competitive.

"You've done some homework since then."

"Yes."

"Good for you. Well. Not until Sitchin published his first translations in a series of books did anyone take him seriously. Because what he'd translated revealed precise information on a range of topics that couldn't have been possible to know for a civilization at the beginning stages of its development, since there was no predecessor to follow. You with me so far?"

"I think so."

"Good. Well. Sitchin claimed the Sumerians had detailed knowledge of the planets, and an understanding of complex medical procedures. Where did they get this knowledge? Sitchin claimed all this wisdom had come from a race of people called the Anunnaki, 'those who from heaven to Earth came.' The Bible speaks of the Elohim, which means God, or 'those who came from the sky.' The Qur'an talks of the Djinn, who are said to be made of a smokeless and scorching fire. Like the scorching fire a drone makes upon detonation."

"And the cuneiform from the warehouse?" Ledge asked.

"The one the journalist found?"

"Yes."

"A breadcrumb leading the way to what Sitchin discovered in his work—reference to a tablet embedded in the earth a long time ago that would never be found, and its code never broken, until the people who had planted it came together again."

"You're talking reincarnation."

"I'm talking the reincarnation of a group."

"Have you had direct contact with this tablet? Are you part of this group, Jack?"

"You're missing the point, Paul. You always miss the point."

"Which is?"

"I'm the messenger. That's all I've ever been. The reason you're here is because your son and the others who survived already have had some kind of contact. They're part of that group and are struggling to remember what to do with it. This knowledge is what got me banished all those years ago. As I was in the process to prove it, that secret defense program was dismantled, and there was no longer a place for me. But your son and that journalist, and likely Hashim and the young boy who survived, have been transformed. You had that chance once and turned away."

The spell of denial Ledge had been under all those years had been dissolving since his son's return. He thought being with Dean would ease his guilt for running away. Instead, it placed him right back into the belly of a complex and unshakable force.

59

Bruton sat in his office at the Pentagon. The meeting with Ledge earlier in the week brought back the pain of his son's death. It also made it hard to deny the endless wars in the Middle East as anything but a waste of lives.

Bruton was aware that Dean had been convinced the tablet was in the desert, and that Dean believed it was the secret reason for America's invasion into a land that had no hand in 9/11.

There were many things, including the otherworldly, the American military would never loosen its grip on when it came to the drive for dominance in the world theatre.

Bruton knew that soon after Saddam Hussein was elevated to power in 1979, he started construction on a sophisticated network of underground tunnels and bunkers. These elaborate constructions were said to be motivated by the threat of an Iranian missile strike, but they were designed as a way to access the tablet, when a psychic told Saddam where she believed it was. She was wrong.

Bruton remembered his dread when Dominique's articles first began to crack open a door to the possible deeper cause for the U.S.

invasion. No one outside his inner circle, not even Dominique, had any idea she was writing about the tablet.

While he was more than six thousand miles from the warehouse when the drone hit, something that day had reached out and pulled him toward images of a violent life he'd led before.

This wasn't the first time he'd entertained the reality of a past life. Too many things seemed familiar to him to dismiss as simple déjà vu. For one, the inexplicable comfort he'd had in his seat of power. He'd been able to rise to this position against tremendous resistance. And while he wouldn't admit it to anyone, he'd always believed there was a metaphysical hand that had helped choreograph his rise.

The desert lured many who'd been told precious secrets lay there. Buried for centuries. Telling of powers they could not comprehend, but desired more than life. It brought the most daring and most vain. Few returned.

Bruton had studied the history of archaeological, multinational, and military interests in these lands. He knew Adrien Kurt had been involved in phenomenological events for which the military needed a rational explanation. That's why he'd called him in when no regular channels were producing results in the wake of Julian and Dominique's kidnapping. He trusted Kurt when Kurt wanted to bring in Catherine Book.

Bruton had been a soldier. He'd seen the viscera and scars of war. Dying men pleading with God. He was one of them.

He sank into his chair, desperate to revive the courage he'd deserted. The heat that had burned in Bruton's mind now turned to an icy chill.

He was tossed back to his near-death in the jungles of Vietnam, waiting for life to ebb from him, laying in a pool of blood on the wet jungle ground. He smelled the dampness and death of that day and realized he'd been running from it ever since, running from the unearthly tether that had connected him to the spirits of that jungle rain forest, as he hovered above himself, choosing life. Now, he was faced with another choice—whether or not to be part of whatever message might be deciphered in the tablet.

60

Monday, September 28

Morning light squeezed through the blinds as Isabel surveyed her kitchen. She was struck at how neat and clean it looked. She hadn't noticed in the three days since her sister had arrived that a sense of order had been restored to her apartment, if not her life. Dishes in the sink had been washed and stacked. The fridge had been absolved of food way past their "use by" date and replaced with fresh fruit and greens. The few plants she had were healthier and trimmed. Furniture and cabinets, dusted—Arama's handiwork to help ingratiate herself and her guests into Isabel's life after their unexpected, unwanted arrival. It was one of the controlling things Isabel didn't miss about her sister, clean apartment be damned. She did appreciate she didn't have to do it, but wouldn't give Arama the satisfaction of her thanks.

Isabel hadn't slept much. She'd spent the weekend at the Department of Justice immersed in getting all the documents collated, bound, and ready for trial. She'd thrived on what her mind could uncouple and understand. The hours of due diligence and her expertise in criminal law had brought her to what she thought she'd wanted. Recognition.

In the midst of her career's rise she'd isolated herself from her past, her sister's singular zeal, and from forging any meaningful relationships of her own. But something Arama said pushed its way forward in Isabel's mind: "The uses of the heart are wiser than the most successful uses of the mind." These were slogans that belonged on bumper stickers, but like everything Arama believed, had enough truth to disturb the stubborn mind. Like now. Isabel saw the reciprocal affection among Arama, Vincente. and his daughter, and Isabel's first thought was how she could use Vincente to keep Arama's childlike zeal contained. That's when she saw Jhana-Merise enter the room.

A finger of light from the blinds illuminated Jhana-Merise's eyes. They reminded Isabel of her mother, the brightness she'd had before succumbing to depression and suicide in their town in the shadow of the sacred ruins of Machu Picchu. After her mother's death Isabel saw nothing hallowed in that land. As far as she was concerned the devil rode on those mountain winds, not God. So, she left before the devil found her.

"I know we've put you in a difficult position," Jhana-Merise said, with the composure of one much older than her young years.

"What do you hope will happen here?" Isabel asked. "Arama has spent much of her life living on dreams. I don't imagine you do."

"We're not here on a dream," Jhana-Merise said. "We're here because we're connected."

As a young girl Arama had introduced Isabel to the phenomenon of Ley Lines. These were hypothetical alignments of a number of places of geographical interest, such as ancient monuments and megaliths. It was said a powerful energy traveled through those lines. And like the chakras of the body, each point was connected and affected by what happened along those paths. Arama had told Isabel if you were to draw a line from their town of Cuzco up through a map of the world, one of the cities you'd go through would be Washington, D.C. "In this way we will always be connected," Arama had said. "And you'll always be below me," Isabel had shot back, poking her sister for her misguided uses of enchantment. Isabel had concrete plans. And plans were never accomplished through magic.

Isabel had been picking at a piece of skin on her thumb and now the cuticle was bleeding. She tucked her thumb under her fingers and folded her arms across her chest, as she and Jhana-Merise stood there in the growing sunlight.

She hadn't picked at her skin in a long time. It was something she did often after her mother's death. That's when religion swooped in to soothe the pain, and talked of resurrection, and that one day they would be together again, when all Isabel needed was to scream until the pain exhausted itself. But she didn't scream, and had constructed a career and life as a barrier to that anguish.

But with this young girl before her, and with wisdom beyond her age, Isabel couldn't shake the feeling there were more than Ley Lines that had brought them together.

61

Dominique stared at the text on her computer screen. She'd finished writing another piece for *The Washington Post*, the first since she'd returned from Iraq.

She'd read much about the core from which extremism comes. And wasn't alone in the way she'd examined the paradox of "the two jihads." The lesser, of the sword. The greater, of the soul.

She knew it was a risk to speak of it, as it had been with others who'd dedicated themselves to grasping the causes of this particular brutality, and that there would be those who would take it as a defense of terrorism.

She was about to send it to her editor. But didn't. She had the thought she would show it to Isabel, as a way to introduce her to the possibility of how she might get inside Hashim's head. By sharing her work, she believed it would bring them closer. Because of what Nazir had told her of what the voice said to him in the desert, Dominique believed Isabel was the lawyer she needed to talk to regarding "the girl." Too much had evolved to deny that she had been led to Isabel. She also knew she needed to be strategic, and didn't want to approach the question of the girl in a way that might shut Isabel down, if indeed she was the conduit.

She knew Isabel was curious to get her perspective on the experience with Hashim, and that the prosecution needed to fill gaps in their case in order to expand the portrait of this mass murderer. Perhaps, her article was a way in. And maybe it wasn't meant to be published, but a way to further her bond with Isabel. And so, she sent her a text asking if they might meet again, as there was something she wanted to share.

Dominique was also eager to know what part this "girl," whoever she was, might be playing in the path unfolding before them.

62

Isabel was sitting at the desk in her makeshift office. She finished reading Dominique's article, looked up at her, and then read a few sentences she'd highlighted, aloud.

"'Religious violence rises from a loss of identity and a misguided reading of holy texts. And from restlessness with a God who doesn't seem to care. This lesser jihad comes from rage at a Western vulgarity that humiliates.'"

"Are you trying to make a case for terrorism? Condoning what Hashim did? Condemning it? Besides Islam, you'll be taking on the Jews and Christians, and…"

"I'm not defending or attacking anyone. I'm showing the core that extremism comes from. Evil demands we not distance ourselves from it by making them monsters. In order to write about it I need to embrace it."

"And, do you?"

"I do. But I don't empathize with it."

Dominique had mastered the art of neutrality and picking up vulnerabilities in her interviewees. That's why she was good at her job. Her silences provoked more truth telling than not. She was used to people challenging her points of view. Thrived on it. And, in the judgment and defense that laced Isabel's words, Dominique got how patronizing Isabel could be, which helped her drill deeper in this character before her.

"It was presumptuous of me to show this to you."

"I didn't mean to doubt your patriotism."

Dominique flashed on the Baghdad debriefing after they were rescued in the desert, when the General had his doubts as to her loyalty.

"Too many see the world in black and white, and project their fear and inadequacy on the Other, when we don't even know them, or care to. I know that sounds like blasphemy. But it's important to consider the source. We are not dry bones cast upon the earth, but flesh and blood in search of connection and meaning."

"You remind me of my sister."

Dominique picked up subtle warmth in her voice when Isabel spoke of Arama.

Dominique achieved what she'd planned—to touch the heart of another, and lead them through an uneven land, like she'd been led. It was a manipulation in service of a greater good, and she let the space remain open, to discover more about this young lawyer.

"What happened over there?" Isabel asked.

Dominique was silent, knowing it was Isabel's attempt to shift the conversation.

"I'm sorry. It's none of my business."

"No, it is," Dominique said, aware of the importance of sharing more.

"When I got back, I visited mosques. I wanted to be in rooms steeped in their belief, to feel the carpets on my forehead and feet, and hear the call of pray. I wanted to feel what they felt, or get as close to it as I could."

"Because of what happened in the warehouse?"

"Yes."

"So, you had a religious experience?"

"That's too narrow an explanation."

"What would you call it?"

"I can no longer avert my eyes to things that must be seen."

"You're talking to a lawyer who's based her life in the concrete, provable, immutable world of facts."

"I know. I also see a questioning mind beyond that concrete world. Perhaps your sister has had an influence on you, as I seem to have, since I remind you of her."

"You're clever, Miss Valen."

"Only in that I thought I would give you a perspective on more than one side of a man. More than the common wisdom."

"You haven't shown this to anyone else, have you?"

"Only you."

And while Dominique realized this wasn't the perfect time, she knew there might not be another.

"May I ask you a question, Isabel?"

"Go ahead."

"If I were to ask you about 'the girl,' would that mean anything?"

Isabel's quick intake of breath told Dominique there was more here to unpack.

"I have no idea what you mean."

"As a lawyer, how would you react to the response you just gave me?"

"I'm not on trial here."

"No one is. You can trust me."

Dominique waited. She knew Isabel had something vital to say, and gave her the time and space to say it.

"You seem to have found a way to process what happened to you in the desert, Miss Valen, and have channeled it into examining the core of terrorism."

Another diversion. But Dominique was no longer willing to play along.

"And you? What have you found in your searching?"

Dominique watched Isabel being thrust into revealing something she seemed no longer able to contain.

"My sister believes in miracles. I don't. I believe they're steeped in a manipulative myth that does nothing but placate and anesthetize."

Dominique saw Isabel grappling with something deeper, and pushed her toward it.

"I happen to agree with you. Is your sister in your life now? Is that why these feelings are so raw?"

"Yes. She's in my life now," Isabel said, and turned away.

Dominique could see Isabel was embarrassed. She let the discomfort be. Dominique knew truth would reveal itself in its own way. She saw Isabel stiffen, her head bent back and her gaze went toward the ceiling.

"You need to tell someone what's going on, Isabel. You can't keep whatever it is, inside. Believe me, I've tried. It doesn't work."

There was no sound like what had come into the warehouse, and penetrated Dominique, but what she saw happening to Isabel she knew was creating a space for truth.

"You found something in the warehouse, didn't you?" Isabel asked.

"How do you know that?"

Isabel turned back to her.

Their eyes locked.

"You can trust me."

"Can I?"

"Yes."

Dominique emanated a confidence and love she knew Isabel had been starving for. She saw a vulnerability overwhelm the young woman before her, giving her a glimpse of the young girl she once was—before tragedy struck, and encased her in a fortress of alienation and her own intractable dogma.

Isabel's voice trembled with these words. "I know someone who claims to be able to activate what lies beneath the desert sand."

"The girl?"

"Yes."

Dominique saw Isabel was exhausted, relieved, and terrified to unburden herself of this secret.

Dominique had engendered these confessions in many of those she'd pursued, and questioned in her career ascent. She knew this young woman's ambition to leave the land of her ancestors had left her tattered roots. It had also brought her here. To this place and appointed time.

The thread being pulled through Dominique's life now included Isabel, her sister, the girl, and whoever else she was about to find.

63

"You remind me of my mother," Jhana-Merise said. She was alone with Dominique. Isabel had set up the meeting in her apartment.

"You were five when she died?"

"Yes."

"You have a strong bond with your father because of it."

Jhana-Merise smiled.

"Tell me about your mother."

"To do that I need to tell you about all of us."

Dominique wasn't sure where this was going, but she was spell-bound in the presence of this young girl who had captivated and terrified a lawyer as brilliant and wounded as Dominique.

Jhana-Merise spoke of the course of their collective souls. She spoke of a time in the desert thousands of years ago. Before history caught up with the search for the tablets. Before anyone knew of their existence.

"We were a violent tribe. We come from violence," Jhana-Merise said. "We're responsible for continuing the chain of events that has controlled the world ever since our ancestors took a bone in their hand and realized it was a weapon with the power to kill. But my mother, who was my sister at that time—"

"You're talking reincarnation."

"I'm talking the arc of a soul, which is given many lifetimes to comprehend its purpose. She knew our purpose was to hide and protect this tablet."

"This is an awful lot of esoteric information for one so young."

"I know," Jhana-Merise said, her smile disarming.

"You mentioned tablets. Are there more than one?"

"Yes. But we're responsible for the one in the desert of Mosul."

"And the others?"

"I believe we'll know them in time."

Dominique eased back into the sofa they were sitting on, comforted by this young girl.

Jhana-Merise spoke of how Abd al Hashim, and bin Laden before him, and many before them, were among those who'd been given a chance to transform the world. But they had a different take on what that meant. Others had tried and failed because the world hadn't reached its tipping point.

"Are we at that point now?"

"I don't know. But I know what we've been brought together to do."

"Activate the tablet in the desert?"

"Yes."

"Did your mother talk about all this to you? Is that how you know so much?"

"She made me aware of our history. Of a collective evolution."

"Collective evolution?"

"Yes. *Unus pro omnibus, omnes pro uno*."

Dominique smiled at the intelligence and grace that this young girl possessed.

"Did your mother know you were sisters in a past life?"

"She was the one who told me."

"And your father?"

"He's been a protector in many lives. A knight. A nobleman. A king. A commoner."

"He's aware of this?"

"He's fought it most of his life. He's a humble man. And, yes, he's aware of this and knows why we're here."

Afternoon sunlight scrawled across the maple wood floor like indistinct words, and the scent of roses drifted into the room. Their eyes revealed they were aware the air had become more than it was. And they were becoming more than they had been.

"Isabel said only you can activate the tablet in the desert."

"That's not true. The tablets are made of a vibration we all possess. They are a manifestation of our soul contract. We planted the one in the desert, but died before we were able to offer it to the earth. That's why the stones appeared, as a way-shower. We planted them as well, for we knew we would forget."

"How do we find that tablet?"

"You go back to where you found the stone."

"The warehouse?"

"In the catacombs deep under the desert floor you'll meet that manifestation. We're each part of a greater soul. Fragments. The vibration in the tablets respond to love. Love that comes from a soul that fools no one, including itself. Love is what placed the tablets. Love is what put that stone in your hand."

"And caused an errant bomb not to kill us?"

"Yes. That the four of you survived is a manifestation of the love beneath the violence. It's not the love we've been led to believe. That's what you transformed in the warehouse—like the alchemy that turns base metal to gold. We are base metal, and our souls, threads of gold. This is what crystalized in the warehouse. This is what's happening to us now."

64

Through a text from a friend at the FBI, Julian found out that an agent was missing. When he saw the attached photo of Aaron Ajam, he realized he was "Taliq." Julian would be hard-pressed for a plan to extract Nazir now, as the FBI knew he was the last person to see Ajam alive. Where would Nazir go? Where could he go? Julian was so deep in the shit of this circumstance he poured himself another glass of scotch from a bottle he'd found in the kitchen cupboard of the cottage.

"Why do you drink so much?" Nazir asked, as he entered the room.

Julian glared at him.

"Taliq was an FBI agent. The terrorist cells won't be the only ones after you now."

"Why don't you turn me in, then?"

"Fuck if I know." He downed the scotch and poured another. "Want one?" he asked, offering the bottle and a glass to Nazir, who ignored the offer.

"What did you see in the warehouse?" Nazir asked.

"Don't do therapy on me, okay?"

Julian stormed out of the kitchen.

Nazir followed and cornered him against a wall in the living room.
"Back the fuck off, kid."
The two men stared each other.
"You're a marked man. And I don't know that I can protect you."
"Allah will do what is best."
"Okay. But for now, you got me."

65

Jack Dean used his cane to punctuate his arrival as he moved toward Charles Bruton's office in the Pentagon. Dean was shocked Bruton had asked to meet after all these years, but the truth was, he'd been waiting for this a long time.

"Thanks for coming, Jack," Bruton said, as Dean entered the office.

Bruton closed the door.

The two men stood there, weighted by betrayal and guilt.

"I owe you an apology, Jack. I don't expect you to forgive me for what I did. Ruining your career."

"What was left of it."

"I put the last nail in that coffin and I'm sorry."

"Is that why I'm here? For an apology?"

"In part."

"No thanks."

He turned to leave.

"Jack. Wait. Please."

Dean had one hand on the doorknob; the other gripped his cane like a sword.

"What's the other part?"

"It's about the tablets. What can you tell me about them?"

"You're not wanting to make a fool of me again, are you?"

"No, Jack. I'm not."

"You've talked with Paul Ledge," Dean said.

"Yes."

Bruton listened as Dean talked of how the stones and the tablets, and all like manifestations, were extensions of a greater truth. He talked of succession into higher consciousness. About the masters who guide us, who have ascended to realms where much is clear, much is merged. But people insist on treating it as a game, and believe the dim light of this world is the only reality.

"Bet you these walls never heard talk like this before," Dean said. "From the level of the sacred within you. And, yes, even you, Charles, have that light. From the degree to which you've opened to it, the vibration imbued within the tablet will respond. Will match the degree of truth within the one who beholds it."

Bruton looked at him, puzzled.

"I'm no more 'crazy' now, Charles, than you believed I was. But you asked me here."

"Go ahead," Bruton said.

"We all understand the world from the level we're at. A child is more capable of accessing the worlds between; they just don't have the tools to express it. The message in the tablets is protected. A spiritual 'fail safe,' if you will. For if there's no light, no love in the beholder, the words will be mysterious and incomplete."

"You say this so easy, Jack."

"I've no more tolerance for bullshit, Charles. We know from the minute we're born why we're here. Do you think there's a person alive who believes *this* is everything? But to look at us one would think that's all we believe. We've convinced ourselves of a lie. You're not the first or the last to know about this. That's what I tried to say before you banished me. There are leaders from the West and East who know what's going on. But they're too scared to come forward.

You can help them. You're in a position to. You've been in that position a long time."

Dean's words slammed Bruton against the fear he'd have to walk through one day, and in so doing, leave his comfort.

"Jack. I'm sorry for what I did to you."

"You can undo it by believing me now."

"And, what would that look like?"

"You're going to be asked to arrange passage back to Mosul. I'd find a way to make that happen."

"For whom and why?"

"For Julian and Dominique. Because they can translate the tablet there."

Bruton knew it would be dangerous and duplicitous to send Julian and Dominique back into harm's way. He also knew it needed to be done. Because the president needed to have that information before anyone else.

PART SIX

The Trial

66

Thursday, October 1

After all the considerations and concerns, and knowing there was no way to keep any of this secret, the location of Hashim's trial would be in D.C. The court was set up blocks away from the Capital building. The National Guard and police presence made it look like a war zone. The network trucks and equipment that crowded the perimeter—creating a moat between the courthouse and the swarms of people—turned it into a circus.

The first floor Media Center was packed with journalists from around the world. A cacophony of languages swirled in the air as they worked the room and sent out information as it came in.

The "No Broadcast" rule from the Center had been suspended. The world wanted to know what was happening, and the government, knowing it wouldn't be able to control the flow of information, made certain there was a huge military and police presence in case things went sideways.

The thrum intensified as the convoy approached the courthouse, and the crush of onlookers, dying for a glimpse of the most wanted man in the world, pressed in hundreds deep.

Along the way Hashim had been transferred twice. First, from the Humvee to one of two black Explorers, then from the Explorer to an armored SWAT vehicle. Four military helicopters had picked up the convoy at dawn and followed them into the city, peeling out as the vehicles moved into the underground courthouse garage.

Soldiers weaved around Hashim, three-sixty, as they moved inside the building. They were prepared for anything.

In the elevator going up to the courtroom, Hashim was moved to the back, as a row of four armed agents stood like a wall between him and the elevator doors. Nothing was being taken for granted, outside, or in the building.

67

In the courtroom were a slew of prosecuting attorneys, headed by the Attorney General, William Caulder. Carl Robinson, one of the two defense lawyers who'd visited Hashim in prison, was the only one at Hashim's side.

The jury, a court reporter, and a court artist were the only other civilians allowed here.

Twelve soldiers flanked the courtroom. No journalists were allowed. They'd get reports from the woman assigned to convey the minutes of the trial every hour.

Hashim was brought in. Shackled.

"Your Honor," Robinson said.

"Yes," Judge Littelton said in a sharp burst, as if he were a drill sergeant. He was a stern man. Short cropped gray hair and military bearing.

"Would it be possible to have the prisoner's chains removed, Your Honor?"

Littelton grunted as he stared at Robinson, then Hashim. He motioned for the bailiff to remove Hashim's chains.

The bailiff approached and removed the manacles from Hashim's hands and feet. Hashim rubbed his wrists. They were red and bruised.

"Thank you, Your Honor," Hashim said.

Littelton motioned him to sit. Hashim did.

"Mister Caulder. Your opening statement for the prosecution," Littelton said.

Caulder strode center stage. He was quick and sharp in his delivery.

"Ladies and gentlemen of the jury, the government will prove, beyond a reasonable doubt, that this man, Abd al Hashim, headed an organization that had the means, the motivation, and the desire to kill thousands of Americans, so that at the end of the trial you'll turn in a verdict of 'guilty' on all counts. Thank you."

He went back to his seat.

Littelton scanned the room, observing and discerning the emotional temperature of everyone.

"Mister Hashim, since you've chosen to represent yourself, do you have an opening statement?"

"I do, Your Honor."

"Let's hear it."

All eyes shifted to Hashim as he approached the jury. The twelve soldiers stepped in closer. The jury flinched in unison at their approach.

Littelton motioned the soldiers back.

The jurors held their gaze on Hashim, who was calm and deliberate as he spoke.

"Ladies and gentlemen of the jury. I am sorry for what I've done."

A murmur vibrated in the courtroom.

"I have been misled by a flawed belief. I have misled my people in that belief. And I am guilty of all the charges your government has brought against me."

The jurors were confused by the confession.

"Is this why you surrendered to the FBI? To come here, into my court, and apologize for the thousands of murders you've committed? You believe an apology is what's required? That it's enough?"

"No, Your Honor."

"So tell me. What do you believe is required?"

"A reckoning for all I've done."

"Mister Hashim. It's not just you who's on trial. It's the mentality that has bred you and others like you."

"I know, Your Honor. And I have come to regret all those actions. We're wrong for the blood we've shed. There's nothing I can do to bring those lives back. And for that I'm sorry. When I see our young men giving their lives to jihad I have remorse. I have perpetrated that violence and put my people on an abhorrent path. Hate is a painful journey. It is venom that poisons the self. You cannot create freedom from hate."

The jurors shifted in their seats. They looked at one another. Confounded.

"We're here today to judge you for the crimes you've committed. For the crimes you've set forth. For the conspiracy against the United States. Not to listen to a confession."

"Yes, Your Honor."

"What do you have to say in your defense?"

Hashim seemed no longer a man of bloodshed, but a man of shame.

"I have no defense, Your Honor. I must pay for what I've done."

"Mister Robinson. Approach the bench."

Robinson moved to Littelton.

"Were you aware of this statement beforehand?"

"Not all of it, Your Honor."

"He didn't take any of your advice?"

"None, sir. We had to force him to agree to even have me present."

"Where is Mister Keyser?"

"Uh. He's not feeling well, Your Honor."

"That sounds like cowardice."

Littelton stood.

"I'd like to see you, your client, and only Mister Caulder in chambers. Now. This court will be in recess until further notice."

Littelton slammed down the gavel and left the room. The three men followed.

No one said a word as the lawyers and Hashim got situated in chambers. Hashim remained standing.

Littelton came in. He leaned back against the dark oak desk.

"Mister Hashim."

"Yes, Your Honor."

"As part of this confession you seem so eager to give, are you prepared to provide specific information regarding the workings of Al-Qaeda, ISIS, and other terrorist organizations? What plans for attacks have been made? Locations of cells? Names of those with whom you have worked? With whom you have conspired, here and abroad? Banks? Financiers?"

"What information I have and know is yours, Your Honor."

Littelton told the Marshall to bring the court stenographer into chambers.

He turned back to Hashim.

"Hassan al Banna, founder of the Muslim Brotherhood has said, 'It is the nature of Islam to dominate, not to be dominated, to impose its laws on all nations and extend its power to the entire planet.' I've studied your history, Hashim. So, why should I trust anything you say?"

"I understand it's hard to believe me."

"That's an understatement."

The Marshall escorted the court stenographer in and sat her next to Littelton.

"What information would you like first?" Hashim asked.

"Do you know where and when the next attacks are planned?"

"Yes. But I assume most, if not all, of those plans are being changed since my surrender."

"You're a clever man, Hashim. I don't trust you. And, if I can't trust you, then all of what you say to me is worthless."

"Your Honor. I was a young boy who once dreamed of peace. Those who had inculcated in me a belief, and those to whom I chose to listen, were caught in an ancient barbarity. Once inside that world even ordinary people will commit evil. But what happened to me in the warehouse transmuted that hate, and I came out from that with a different purpose—a soldier who would renounce our violent jihad. Our grievances mask a deep fear. Fear of a godless world, of chaos and loneliness, fears we all have. They also mask greed for power, land, and money. A type of masculine wound America knows well. I was taught to intensify these needs in order to ignite holy war."

Littelton peered at Hashim a long time. It made the others restless.

"You're a smart man, Hashim. Tell me. What about the others? Did they transform from this near-death experience?"

"I don't know, sir."

"You've had no contact with them since the warehouse?"

"No," Hashim said, lying to protect them.

"Your purpose in sneaking into this country wasn't to finish what you'd started there?"

"No, sir."

"What about the woman, Catherine Book? The CIA told me about her."

"I know nothing of her."

"These individuals seem to have had an intimate experience of you and yet you know nothing of them?"

"The journalist and the soldier were in the warehouse with me. I wanted to kill them. That experience is not a basis for attachment. I'm told Catherine Book has some special ability, of which I know nothing."

"What about the young boy, Nazir Siraj? He was in the warehouse with you."

"I left him with his grandmother in Mosul. He was injured in the explosion."

"You've not seen him since?"

"No, Your Honor."

The two men studied each other.

"Do you know Sayyid Sarif?"

"Not personally."

"Well, the FBI raided the local terrorist cell he fronted here in D.C., but no one was there. Do you know who might have warned him? Where he might be now?"

"I can conjecture where he might be now."

"Then do that."

"There's a farm in Pennsylvania used as a safe house. I don't know the address but if you give me a map I will point the area out for you."

"Get me a detailed map of the state of Pennsylvania," Littelton said to the Marshall.

68

Under cover of night, ten FBI agents made their way up the long dirt drive to a two-story red brick farmhouse on the outskirts of Pennsylvania.

SWAT, and an army of back up, waited behind the dense foliage surrounding the property. Drones had transmitted heat signature images of three persons inside the main house. The silo to the left was abandoned and empty.

One of the agents placed a charge by the front door, the others surrounded the house.

The charge exploded, the front door shattered, and within that noise rapid gunfire came from inside the house, but it wasn't enough to stop the fusillade of return fire.

The agents made their way in as SWAT and backup followed.

The three inside were dead, their bodies riddled with bullets. The agents took fingerprints and sent the information back to FBI headquarters in D.C.

Within a few minutes they received confirmation that one of the men was Sayyid Sarif.

PART SEVEN

The Cave of Memory

69

Saturday, October 3

The transport flight Bruton had put Julian and Dominique on landed in Joint Base Balad at dawn. It was in the Sunni Triangle forty miles north of Baghdad. That left the remaining 180 miles to Mosul for them to travel.

The cab was thick with sweet licorice. "Yansoun," the cabbie said when Dominique asked what the scent was. "Aniseed. Anise." He spoke through more gums than teeth. "It is one of oldest spices from Egypt." And it hung on him like perfume.

A CD played music from cracked speakers. The singer's voice was beautiful.

Dominique asked what it was. The cabbie lit with joy. "The Qur'an," he said.

It reminded her of the prayer Hashim had chanted in the warehouse.

Julian took her hand as they came into the city. Mosul held a dark memory. Nazir had given Julian the name of the one who'd helped him escape. The same man who'd forged the Nicolas Sandor passport for Hashim. His name was Ja'far.

That night, Julian and Dominique waited in a café in a corner of the bazaar. The brilliant colored fabrics that billowed as the soft night wind blew captivated Dominique. The scent of dried herbs and teas rode on the air from the stalls of merchants closing their shops.

This was a land of magic, she thought, as she breathed in the sweet-scented intoxicant air and stood among the fabrics that seemed so full of life. She remembered a line from Milton's *Paradise Lost*: "Millions of spiritual creatures walk the earth unseen, both when we wake, and when we sleep." She'd always believed literature captured a level of unseen reality. And here, in this place, she knew the air itself was animate with these spirits.

She broke from her reverie when a weathered man with a wisp of beard approached them at the café.

Dominique stared at him. He looked familiar.

"I know, I know," Ja'far said, with a twinkle and a smoker's rasp. "Everyone says I look like your actor, John Hurt."

"He's English," Dominique said with a grin.

"There's a difference?" Ja'far said, winking. "Allah rest his soul."

He handed Dominique a piece of paper. Written upon it was a password Nazir had told them he would provide in order to confirm his identity.

Dominique handed the paper to Julian, who looked at it, tore it up and said, "Okay."

Ja'far went right to business and began to lay out the plan for the morning. He would pick them up at the hotel before dawn. Together they would travel outside the city to an underground access point into the cave of memory.

For Dominique, time past and time present had merged. What time future would bring she had no idea.

70

Sunday, October 4

The battered pickup truck Ja'far drove was thick with the smell of herbs and gunpowder. The scent of war had soaked into every fabric of his life. There'd been no escape from the contagion. He maneuvered through the sleepy back alleys of Mosul into the cold dawn of the desert—toward the cave he'd told them was their destination.

In the back seat, Dominique held tight to Julian's hand. The last time they'd been transported out of this town was with tape on their mouths and burlap over their heads, going to their death. And while she had no certainty them going back to the warehouse to find the tablet precluded that danger, she also felt the protection of the millions of spiritual creatures who walked the Earth unseen. And, as if Ja'far had read her mind, he spoke of those creatures.

"Islam explains the world of the Djinn."

Through the front windshield, an aurora brushed traces of red and green streams of morning light on the road before them.

"Islam provides us with many answers to the mysteries of things seen and unseen."

Ja'far had a theatrical flair.

"The Djinn are beings created with free will, living on earth in a world parallel to ours. They are invisible to us. This makes it easy to deny their existence, but their origins can be traced from the Qur'an and the Sunnah. The Djinn were created from fire, and they live in the deserts and wastelands. They were created before man. Before the angels. Allah speaks of this. And God does not lie." He caught Julian peering at him in the rearview. "What it is?" Ja'far asked.

"You speak English very well."

"Since I was a child many foreigners have come to this land. Especially the British."

"The Anglo-Iraqi war."

"Yes. I was five years old in May of 1941 when they re-occupied The Kingdom of Iraq."

"You're not that old."

"Oh, yes I am. But don't let my age distract you from my youthful heart, my sharp mind, and my expert abilities. I knew even at five that I must learn to speak the language of the enemy."

"Yet, you're being helpful to us," Dominique said, charmed by him.

"In the hope of what we find, and what you're able to decipher, that you will remember this kindness and know we're not all savages. And use it to help more than yourselves."

"That we will, Ja'Far," Dominique said.

"Good. Because you will discover much more than you believe possible."

They were on the edge of town when Ja'far ran out of words. He stopped the pickup. Took a crumpled pack of Mikado cigarettes from his jacket pocket and jumped out of the truck.

"Wait," Julian said, following him out.

He pulled out a pack of Marlboros from his jacket pocket and handed it to Ja'far.

"These are much better than that crap."

"Thank you," Ja'far said with a smile. He took a Marlboro from the pack; Julian did the same and offered one to Dominique, who passed.

Ja'far rolled his thumb down the wheel of a battered Zippo and took a drag of the smoke. He lit Julian's cigarette.

"Hashim's grandfather, Qadir, told me what happened to Hashim," Ja'far said. "They spoke in a dream."

"A dream?" Julian said.

"Yes. Do you not dream?"

"I dream," Julian barked, and turned away.

"Did Qadir tell you what they spoke of?" Dominique asked.

"He told me about the butterfly and the words Hashim saw written in the air. And of the ground that stopped opening beneath you. Is that not what happened?"

"Let's move on," Julian said, making his way back to the truck.

"Wait," Ja'far said.

Julian stopped, impatient.

Ja'far finished his smoke as a dot of cinnamon sun bled through the hot, grey haze of the desert. He crushed the cigarette butt with his heel into the sand. He grabbed a heavy satchel from the trunk.

"We walk from here."

They walked for hours before arriving at a massive gravesite long since abandoned. The sun disappeared with a puff behind the horizon line. The temperature dropped and the air turned cold.

Ja'far led them down an unsteady ladder to the lowest surface of the site.

In the growing moonlight they walked through bleached bones and weather-shattered trinkets left as prayers.

"The terror began here long before Saddam," Ja'far said.

They reached a wall at the far edge of the site.

Ja'far studied the moon.

"What are you doing?" Julian asked.

"Waiting," Ja'far answered.

"For what?" Dominique said.

"The moon will guide us."

Dominique and Julian moved to a patch of ground away from the bones.

Ja'far took the heavy satchel he'd been carrying, tossed it on the ground, opened it, and from inside took out a chunk of coal. He made a small pit, nestled the coal inside it and lit the coal with his Zippo. The coal took the flame, drew it in, and began to give off its warmth. Ja'far sat in front of the pit. Dominique and Julian did the same.

"Are we going to be here a long time?" Julian asked.

"Until the moon allows us to enter the cave."

Julian raised the collar of his jacket and moved to the other end of the gravesite.

Dominique and Ja'far sat in the quiet of the desert night, Ja'far's attention on the arc of the moon.

Dominique studied Ja'far. In the glow of the coal heat there was something about him that looked familiar, beyond the echo of John Hurt.

In the week since she'd met Jhana-Merise, Dominique couldn't stop thinking about her—about one of the things she'd said: "we are base metal and our souls are threads of gold."

Ja'far was another thread being pulled through their lives. And while the idea of reincarnation wasn't foreign to her, she'd come to a deeper understanding since that meeting, when Jhana-Merise said Dominique reminded her of her mother.

Dominique had contacted the friends she'd made in Cuzco. The same friends who'd told her of the miracle of the boy in the burn unit. She'd asked them to see if they might be able to find any information on Vincente Salva's wife, Jhana-Merise's mother. What they found brought Dominique to another level in their collective evolution.

The mother's name was Daniela. She worked for a time as a guide at Machu Picchu. She was well-known for telling stories of the entities that lived in the mountains there. She had the reputation for speaking truth to power, not unlike Dominique's quest in her work.

Dominique had heard of split souls—souls with a power so huge they needed more than one personality within which to bring forth their purpose—the same soul that needed to occupy more than one human being in any given lifetime. There were even souls that had many splits. Could it be that each of those on this journey were part of the same soul? Was this the insight to which they were being led?

"We've been here before, haven't we?" she asked Ja'far.

A sweet, orange wind stirred through the ancient killing field. The scent jolted Dominique's memory back to an earlier time. A time of rescue, and ointments Bedouin had used to heal her when she was dying in the desert of an earlier life. It was this fruit she smelled, and this life she saw.

"It was you who helped me," she said in calm awe. "They were your hands that applied the ointments that cured me."

"Yes. I was one of the tribe who took care of you here. Inside this place is where you were saved."

"The Cave of Memory," she said, remembering when she'd walked in the monotone of the desert, from a land to which she'd been banished. Walking upon sand with this tribe of which Ja'far had been part. The same sand she and Julian had walked on in their escape from the desert. The same sand that was on her bare feet in the cold of that night when they were saved. She'd been saved in many lives. Now it was her turn to save others.

"Yes. We have been here before," Ja'far said.

The arc of the warm cream moon illuminated an unseen opening along a vertical line of rock.

Ja'far moved his hands along the surface of the rock, along a seeming invisible line until he opened it enough for a human being to move through.

Julian approached him, curious as to what he was doing. He saw the opening.

"Did you move that rock?"

"It wasn't me alone. Now we must go inside."

Ja'far took out a small flashlight from his pocket and squeezed through the portal in the rock.

Julian and Dominique followed.

The scent of roses seeped from the pores of the ancient cave.

Dominique remembered…

She was being dragged across dry riverbeds on a boat made of sticks. Bedouin cocooned and covered her in oil moist leaves to protect her burned skin from the sun. She was brought into the cool of a cave she heard the Bedouin call, The Cave of Memory. Night came. A fire warmed against the desert rime. A story was told as flames glimmered on the cave walls of an earlier time. The eldest of the tribe anointed her eyes and skin with more ointments. They knew well of healing, these desert people. But what great realm had summoned them to save her?

"It was as if you were placed there by God," Dominique said. She saw Julian and Ja'far looking at her, as her experience traveled from the cave then, to now.

"Are you all right?" Julian asked.

"She's remembering what happened here a thousand years ago," Ja'far answered.

Dominique saw that Julian was frightened and doubting. But he was here.

Ja'far led Dominique and Julian through a maze of catacombs. They'd been walking for hours and stopped to rest. Dominique asked how much farther they needed to go. Ja'far told her that while the entrance point was the burial ground they'd come from, it wasn't the location of the tablet. The catacombs would take them to under the abandoned warehouse many miles away from where they started. So, if they were followed, no one would be able to find the entrance through the rock they'd entered.

"And if by some chance they were able to find it?" Julian asked.

"They wouldn't survive in the catacombs."

"Why not?"

"Because we're very deep under the ground."

"What about the air? How will we breathe when we get there?" Dominique asked.

"We're breathing now, and we're already hundreds of feet under the desert."

"What are you talking about? How is that possible?" Julian demanded.

"How is any of what's happened to you possible?"

Dominique saw that Julian was having a hard time buying this.

"We've got to come to the surface at some point. Or are you planning to keep us here?"

"When we've done what we came to do, we will go back to the surface."

"I'm fucking glad you're that confident."

"I am," Ja'far said. And he told them of the stories handed down for centuries. Stories that gave his tribe the knowledge to be guides and guardians. And with that wisdom came the ability to channel a vibration that would illuminate the tablet in the darkness of the catacombs—a vibration in those who had been given the task to lead others here. Ja'far came from such a tribe, and Dominique and Julian were for whom they had been waiting. He knew about them. About their lives, their childhoods. He told her something she'd never shared with anyone: how during her near-death in that hospital room in

Pittsburgh, the young Dominique saw herself as an adult and knew she would survive. "*The Two Dominiques* you called it."

"How did you know that?"

"The desert has revealed many things to our tribe. It's how we survived."

Ja'far also knew of the young girl from Cuzco.

Something flashed in the distance.

"What's that?" Dominique asked, startled.

"It's white rock. Quartz that glimmers when it catches the light."

"Where's the light coming from?" Julian asked.

"Welcome to the guardian of the tablet," Ja'far said, pointing proudly to himself.

They made their way toward the light at the end of the tunnel. They reached what seemed like a dead end and stood before a translucent wall.

Julian touched the wall and pulled away.

"Don't be afraid. It's testing your DNA," Ja'far said. "It wants to be sure you are who you are supposed to be."

"Am I?"

"Not yet, I'm afraid."

Dominique touched the wall. She didn't pull away. She felt a language in its pulse.

If she had to explain merging with the vibration in the wall… words failed. It was called a tablet, what she pressed her hand into, but there was nothing written on it.

Searing heat ripped through her body and she clenched in the pain.

Julian rushed to her.

Ja'far stood in his way.

Julian shoved him aside.

"Stop," Dominique shouted.

Her voice rippled through the tunnels of the catacomb like the wrinkles a flat rock makes skipping over water on its endless glide.

The sound traveled like it would never end. That's when they realized it was no longer the echo of her voice that filled the air.

The sound was coming from the tablet.

Dominique remembered what Kurt had said about the sound love makes traveling through time. Was this that sound?

"Yes," Ja'far said in answer to her thought.

The sound carried with it the pain of centuries. The pain she'd caused. The pain inflicted on her. That she was strong enough to absorb the horror, and transmute it to what she could only call the love beneath, brought forth from this mysterious wall an energy that penetrated her with words. They were: "Evil is the greatest source of transformation."

Julian watched as she seemed almost to become one with the wall, which throbbed. And the air smelled like honey.

"What the fuck is going on?" Julian said.

Ja'far raised his hand in a gesture to Julian that said, *listen*.

Julian stilled himself and took in the sound. His breathing calmed, and his body quieted.

"What's happening?" Julian asked.

"We're constructing a portal from the darkest side of our soul to the light," Ja'far answered.

71

Catherine listened to Nazir as he spoke of having traded angels for devils. They were in the garage of her cottage. He was helping her clean the furnace, for a cold front was moving in, and she needed to be certain there'd be heat for what might be a long stay. Julian had asked her to be with Nazir until he and Dominique came back from where they were going and could figure out what to do with him. They didn't tell Catherine they were in the desert. But she knew.

The furnace kicked on. Nazir jumped at the sudden sound.

"It's the heater. There's nothing to be afraid of."

He moved toward its warmth.

She could see he had something on his mind.

"What is it?" she asked.

He moved away. Disquieted.

"You can trust me, Nazir."

He sat on one of the wooden boxes. On top of a stack of books, next to the box, he saw a photograph of a handsome young man. He didn't take his eyes off the photo.

"He's my son. His name is Scott."

"Where is he?"

"He died years ago."

Except for Hashim, she hadn't been back to the cottage since Scott's death here. She'd never wanted to come back. She'd tried to sell it, but something always interfered.

"How did he die?"

She was reluctant to reveal the truth, because she knew Nazir's world looked upon homosexuality with rabid fury. But she was compelled to speak.

"Complications caused by the AIDS virus. Do you know what that is?"

"Yes."

She could see this was a scary level of intimacy for him. But Nazir was a young man, far from home, and she was still a mother.

She sat next to him on another wooden box. He didn't move away.

"When did you first meet Hashim?" she asked.

"I've known him ever since I can remember. He was my teacher and my friend."

"What was it like when they asked you to track him down here?"

"I'd been betrayed before. Suspicion and doubt are part of our lives."

"But you trusted him for so long."

"Yes. But trust can be dangerous."

That he could doubt his mentor, to the extent of thinking he might be a traitor, surprised Catherine.

She thought of the poem Hashim had given her, the tender poem he'd written when he was a boy. And she remembered what Dominique had said to her about first seeing Nazir in the warehouse—that if jihad was attracting young men this sensitive it meant there was much more to fear than anyone could imagine. What was it about their sensitivity that turned them to violence, and gave way to this mistrust? Wasn't the ability to feel deeply a deterrent from cruelty and doubt, not a catalyst?

"How can you be suspect of someone this close to you?"

He folded his arms and turned away. She could see he was shamed by the question.

"I'm not judging you, Nazir. I want to know. I want to understand."

When he stood she saw a shift in him, and wasn't sure what it meant. But she wasn't going to be afraid.

"My mistrust of Hashim feels like betrayal. Because what he taught me was the opposite of what had come before—that we young are lost, humiliated, alienated, and looking for a place to put our rage. Hashim came from love. That is why so many of us followed him."

"But that love killed."

"Doesn't the God of your faith allow people to die horrendous deaths? And doesn't that same God come from love?"

His words pushed her right back into the mournful memory of her son, and his harrowing death.

She cried.

"I'm sorry. I didn't mean to make you sad."

"It wasn't you."

She reached her hand out to him.

He held it.

"You've been kind to me. But I can't stay. This is not where I belong."

"Where will you go?"

"Allah will show the way."

72

Nazir walked in the dark chill of a D.C. morning. His thoughts of finding a mosque for refuge evaporated in the fear of being recognized and caught. So, he sought refuge inside a church.

Morning Mass was in progress.

He crossed a border into a new land, foreign and forbidding.

He slipped into a pew to not draw attention.

An invisible pressure on his shoulder made him look across the aisle. A young girl smiled at him. She was sitting alongside an older man and a woman. Nazir thought he'd been discovered. Panic flushed through him.

"Stay," Jhana-Merise whispered from across the aisle. Nazir looked around for signs of danger. All he saw were worshippers, heads bowed.

Jhana-Merise tiptoed to him and sat by his side.

Arama touched Vincente's hand. It stopped him from motioning his daughter back.

"You're safe with us," Jhana-Merise said, nodding in the direction of her father and Arama.

Nazir was still unsure.

A sweet perfume hung in the air. He searched for the source of the thick smell.

"It's incense," she said. "It's not the same as the roses."

"You know about the roses?"

"Yes. I'm the girl you told Dominique to ask the lawyer about. The same girl you heard the voice in the desert speak to you of."

Nazir had no idea how this all was being played out, or where it would end. He did know the energy that entered the warehouse after the drone hit, had infused him with a knowledge he had no way to possess on his own. He knew he was an integral part of what was unfolding. That he was drawn to a church, this church, was another way he was being led.

As Mass continued, he listened to Jhana-Merise talk of the stones and the tablet and the history of what they shared.

She told him that many have written about tablets, from Plato to Isaac Newton. That much had been written about cuneiforms and tablets and sacred texts. But none have written about the tablet in the desert, because that tablet is a void, a portal, and only those who'd planted it can activate it, for the tablet may only be initiated through the love of those responsible for its existence.

"We did not create it," she said, "but we are the consciousness through which it will arrive. And what that consciousness will reveal will neither be easy to understand and accept, nor safe. It will confront the reality we've been anesthetized to believe."

The Mass continued, all eyes on the altar. But they were in their own world.

Nazir spoke of a story his mother told him when he was a boy, about a secret red door. A secret door he would find one day and be offered the chance to go through. If he went through, he would remember who he was and wouldn't be alone, for there were others who would remember, too, and be offered the same choice. He always believed that door was the red door Hashim had led him through in the safe house in Mosul when he was twelve, to learn the ways of his mentor.

"Did your mother tell you who you would remember you were?" Jhana-Merise asked.

The bells from the altar rang for communion.

"No. I always asked her, and she always told me I would know when the time came."

Jhana-Merise took his hand and said, "The time has come."

73

Isabel was startled when she entered her apartment. Not only were her sister, Jhana-Merise, and Vincente here, but Nazir was also standing in her living room. She recognized him from the photos she'd compiled for the DOJ's case against Hashim.

The pressure she'd been under, not only the quandary of what to reveal of Jhana-Merise's presence and her knowledge of Hashim, but the intense preparation and secrecy for the trial had affected her performance. She'd been reprimanded for letting slip some classified discovery materials to a member of the defense team who hadn't obtained the requisite security clearance. Since the trial had ended when Judge Littelton brought Hashim to chambers she'd been relegated to other work outside the DOJ's purview. She was intent on working her way back into their graces. But the presence of Nazir in her apartment brought a new terror.

"He can't stay here," Isabel said to Arama.

The sorrow in Arama's eyes was something Isabel knew well from their life in Cuzco. And, Isabel read in Vincente's regretful smile awareness that he and his daughter had overstayed their welcome.

"I'm sorry. There's too much at stake for me to have you here."

"Don't abandon us. You did that when you left father and me after mother died. Don't make your ambition and fear what the rest of your life is about."

The shame that Isabel had sequestered in her rise to what she believed was greater than the blood that ran through her ripped open.

Arama held her sister as she sobbed.

74

The setting orange sun shred its way in through jagged walls as seven mujahideen walked amid the rubble of the warehouse. The crushing desert heat, fallen blocks of stone, and metal had charred and pulverized the bodies of Hashim's insurgents who didn't survive the explosion three weeks before.

Rumors of the newly found cuneiform by the Americans had brought them here.

As they searched through the ruins for more stones, they heard the engines of Jeeps move toward the warehouse. Seconds later, mortars and grenades exploded and white phosphorus filled the air.

In suicide mode, three of the mujahideen rushed toward the Americans, firing a blast of bullets as they came into the warehouse—killing two of the five Special Forces. In turn, those three mujahideen were ripped apart when the other three Special Forces sent a mortar screaming down the hall. The other mujahideen scattered.

The Special Forces tracked them through the rubble.

On the young leader's signal, they sent in a barrage of mortars.

The walls of the hall collapsed.

They heard the screams of dying men.

The mujahideen were buried alive.

The violence settled.

The taste of metal, and the smell of burning flesh filled the air, as the Special Forces made their way through the rubble to make sure all mujahideen were dead.

Outside the warehouse, the commander radioed base camp and told them the targets had been eliminated.

Word came back from the Pentagon to stay put because there would be more mujahideen on the way, as well as backup Special Forces.

"We're protecting much more than three people in the catacombs," Bruton told the commander.

75

Monday, October 5

Catherine Book sat in Bruton's office at the Pentagon. It was the first time they were in the same room. After Hashim had kidnapped Julian and Dominique in Mosul, Bruton tasked Kurt to enlist Catherine to find them. He needed her to find them again.

"Why did they go back to the warehouse?"

Bruton unlocked a drawer. He took out a dark velvet bag and placed it on the desk.

"Can you tell me what's in this bag?"

"I'm not a dog who does tricks."

"I didn't mean to insult you."

"You did."

He went to unwrap it.

"It's a cuneiform," she said, before she even saw it.

He opened the bag and handed her the stone.

"This is from the warehouse?"

"Yes."

"If you know they're there why do you need me?"

"Because, they're in the catacombs deep underneath."

"And don't have a way out?"

"We don't have a way to communicate with them and we need a way in."

"Who's we?" she asked.

"There's a Special Forces team above ground waiting for instructions. I need you to find a way in for them, so we can let the three in the catacombs know it's us coming in, and not the enemy, and get them out safely—before more mujahideen arrive and find them, and the tablet, because they will."

76

The Special Forces team positioned themselves along the eastern wall of the warehouse. They'd found an indentation in the foundation of the building and began to dig.

Bruton had sent them an electronic drawing of Catherine Book's remote view rendering of a possible access point into the catacombs, as well as a drawing of the catacombs themselves that would lead them to Julian and Dominique.

Due to the depth they'd need to go, and the constricted breadth of the drop to get there, two of the leaner members of the team were chosen.

"You haven't told your wife where you are, have you?" the commander said with a wink to the first soldier strapping on equipment.

"No, sir. She thinks I'm in Hawaii, sir."

The guys laughed.

"That's good, Murphy. She should never know where you are unless you're in her bed."

"Yes, sir. I hope to be there soon, sir. We plan to have a bunch of kids, sir."

"And you're good to go, too, Wilson?" the commander asked the second soldier.

"Yes, sir," Wilson said.

"You planning on a family?"

"No, sir. I prefer more than one bed to lie in."

The guys hooted.

Murphy and Wilson finished putting on the specialized scuba equipment, which made them look like a cross between fire fighters and deep-sea divers—with rigs, harnesses, and cylinders of high-pressure breathing gas weighing down on their bodies.

As Catherine predicted, the ground gave way at one of the access points where they dug.

One of the soldiers pointed his flashlight into the opening, but all he could see was darkness. He dropped a piece of stone from the destroyed warehouse and listened.

After a few seconds there was a splash. With one end of a seemingly endless rope ladder secured to the front of the Jeep, another soldier unfurled the other end of the ladder into the void.

Murphy made his way first down the ladder. Wilson followed. The others remained on the surface and kept watch.

When they reached bottom, Murphy and Wilson followed the maze-like stretch of Catherine's instructions.

These men knew of Julian's bravery during the height of the devastating insurgent attacks in Fallujah. They knew how many of their own he'd risked his life for and saved. This knowledge grounded them in the purpose of their assignment in the tunnels. One of their own needed protection, and they would do whatever they could to keep him, and those with him, safe and alive.

They stopped when they heard a hum at the end of a long tunnel.

"Captain Ledge," Wilson called. His voice echoed.

No answer. Just the hum.

It was then they noticed the sweet smell of roses. They were confused, as their air was self-contained in the high-pressure breathing masks they wore that prevented the exterior atmosphere from entering. They pushed their confusion aside and searched for the source, but there was no clear emanating point. It seemed to come from all around them as if the rock exhaled the scent.

"What the fuck is going on here?" Wilson said.

"I don't know," Murphy replied. "But it's weird. Stay alert."

A cautious worldview is the best insurance in a risky, uncertain world. But faced with an unknown danger—especially one with the paranormal complexity with which Wilson and Murphy were being presented—their military minds were being coupled with the transcendent nature of what was manifesting before them.

In this mystery, they were being led by the fragrance of roses, as they made their way down a seemingly endless tunnel.

They came upon an opening, through which they saw movement.

Cautious and hyper-focused, they flanked the opening, identified who they were, and called Julian's name. When Julian called back, they knew they'd reached their target.

Julian helped them through the opening, where they saw Dominique and Ja'far. It was here they realized the hum was coming from the wall in front of them, and the scent of roses was its strongest.

The wall pulsed in a way that seemed to make it alive. That's when they realized the three they'd come to rescue were breathing on their own.

Wilson was about to remove his mask. Julian grabbed his hand and ordered him to stop.

Ja'far stepped in and said it was all right. He helped the soldiers remove their masks.

Murphy took deep breaths. "What the fuck?"

"What the hell is going on?" Wilson said, able to breathe.

"There's a source of air that comes in from the fissures here," Ja'far said, lying to quell their questions. "But let's not press our luck and stay too long."

"Let's get the hell out of here," Murphy said. "There's more mujahideen on the way. We gotta go now."

"Not the way you came," Ja'Far said.

Murphy and Wilson weren't about to take orders from a stranger.

"We'll follow Ja'Far," Julian ordered. "He knows the way out."

"We won't be able to breathe once we're out of this area," Wilson said.

"Don't worry," Ja'Far answered. "I know where all the fissures are."

"Who is this guy?" Murphy asked.

"He's the guy who's going to get us out alive," Julian answered.

77

After traveling all night, Dominique, Julian, and Ja'far arrived in Baghdad. They each were taken to separate debriefs.

These brass were less fueled by suspicion than the debriefs a month earlier after what had happened in the warehouse.

Dominique pleaded for the release of Ja'far in her debriefing. But in spite of her protests that he was on their side and had guided and protected them, the military wasn't ready or willing to let go of a local who might have information that could prove useful.

"You're so fucking paranoid it's made you deaf, dumb, and blind." Dominique spit out her words. But they had no effect on the unbending brass.

78

Julian tasted blood that wasn't his own. A young girl, who looked much like Jhana-Merise, stared at him. Helpless. Waiting. They were in the desert of another war. Dead bodies around them. A sword his weapon.

A sandstorm approached, and the surface of the desert rose as if responding to an unseen mammoth force beneath. The sky was shut out. Everything faded from his view except the girl who clung to him.

A wall of darkness hurtled toward them.

Julian drew his sword, ready to attack the wind. It hit with the force of a tsunami but he didn't let go of the girl even as he was battered to his knees.

The sand became a blanket of death and buried them.

Julian was startled out of his sleep.

Rain thrummed on the windows of the local hotel the government had put them up in.

"You all right?" Dominique asked.

Heart pounding, Julian told her about the dream.

"What you experienced was a door to the past," Dominique said. "A way to help us change the future."

He touched her face with a tenderness that filled her eyes with tears.

"I remembered something when we were in the catacombs," he said.

"What?"

The memory made him anxious. He got out of bed and paced the room.

"It's about my father. I'd always wondered what it was that had terrified him when I was a boy. It terrified my mother, too. That's when she began to drink hard."

"What did you remember there?"

"My father was in the catacombs with me. I could feel him. Feel a sorrow. A longing for something out of reach."

The rain gave a gentle healing, and opened Julian to a deeper level of connection with his father.

"He had an experience once like we did and turned away. And it's haunted me ever since, although I didn't know it until the catacombs. I've turned away from so much, I've become like him."

"You're changing that."

It was his eyes that now filled with tears.

79

The second wave of mujahideen were too focused on their greed to realize the approaching swarm of flies, and the haze that darkened the sky, were a portent. Three Jeeps were filled with warriors on a mission to conquer the tablet.

Many of their armies had perished over the centuries pursuing desert treasures. Ancient warriors who searched for better lives. And while some had found ways to heal the hunger, the violence continued, and the desert was bled of hope.

But into this world the prophet Muhammad came. Orphaned and later discontented, he retreated to a cave where an angel appeared in a vision, giving the first of the revelations that could save them.

Those words moved some to lay down swords. But not all. For they held tight to their right of dominion over this land.

These mujahideen were holding tight still, even as the sand leapt in spirals, swirling, smothering the black shroud of flies.

A tidal wave of sand shut out the sky, as the Jeeps sped even faster toward their goal—the warehouse—hoping for refuge. But before they could reach it they were suffocated in the avalanche of desert sand and buried alive.

History has recorded the death of various armies engulfed in poisonous storms, never to be seen again. Some had even declared war on these tempests and marched out in full battle array, only to be interred.

This was the fate of misguided, hubristic men bent on destruction. Men with whom Julian had once been connected, in a lifetime long ago.

The desert would continue to consume all those who would come to conquer this treasure. It would wait for those whose vibrations would release it.

80

Monday, October 12

Bruton escorted Dominique through the halls of the Pentagon. Her curiosity peaked as they made their way to a stark basement area. Grey concrete walls. Harsh fluorescent lights. Soldiers at attention like blocks of ice.

Bruton whispered, “You really believe there’s spiritual DNA?”

She stopped and looked at him. She could see he was anxious.

“Yes, I do.”

“And that the missile I sent to Hashim’s village had a mind of its own and meant for all this to happen?”

“Einstein called it, ‘spooky action at a distance.’ But I’m confused. I thought you were on board with all this.”

“I am. But when we get into the world of quantum entanglements we have to tread lightly. Not everyone will be willing to entertain the possibilities.”

“You’re making this very mysterious.”

"It is," he said, and proceeded down cement stairs through another hallway, to a door at the end.

Dominique followed on high alert.

Being here, and the mystery of all that had engaged her imagination with excitement, turned to trepidation at the ominous door at the end of the hall.

Bruton opened the door to a bunker-like room with a round table and six chairs. Standing behind the chair at twelve o'clock was the President of the United States. His elegant black suit and dark blue tie framed his round, intense face. He was taller than she imagined.

Dominique was speechless and scared. She had no idea if she was about to be whisked away to some black site.

"Thank you for coming, Miss Valen," the president said as he reached out his hand. She thought it was for a handshake. Instead, in his hand was a cuneiform. It had symbols carved in it different from the stone she'd found in the warehouse.

She was curious how it came to be in his possession, but was too afraid to say anything.

"Take it," he said.

Her hand trembled. She took the stone from him.

The room filled with the scent of roses.

The president and Bruton regarded each other.

Dominique couldn't tell if it was awe, fear, or dread.

"Did the other cuneiform you touched produce this same result?"

"Yes, sir."

This was another rabbit hole, the depth of which she had no idea. But she was relieved she wasn't the only one who could smell the roses here.

She didn't know if this was an inquiry or interrogation.

She studied the distinctive stone in her hand. Its throbbing pushed away her fear.

"Where did you get this?" she asked.

"You're not the first to come upon the stones, Miss Valen. But you've unleashed more than the scent of roses. Now, ISIS is bent on getting to them no matter how many mujahideen or Americans are sacrificed. They believe infidels have gained access to what is theirs, and they'll stop at nothing to get back what's been taken from them. We are on their land. And have found what they couldn't."

Dominique looked at Bruton, wondering where this was going.

"Mister Bruton has told me what you've told him about the stones, and the tablet with which you've made contact. But if there's anything else we need to know before you leave here, tell me now."

She knew she needed to come clean if she hoped to have the force of the White House behind her.

"There is more, sir. The language of the tablet in the desert is a language of energy."

"How so?" the president said, folding his arms.

"We were hundreds of feet under the surface of the warehouse in the catacombs, and were able to breathe on our own."

"Yes, Charles told me. Even the Special Forces."

"Yes, sir. But we told them the air came in through fissures in the rock."

"And they believed you?"

"They didn't ask questions, but I imagine they had them."

"What does this have to do with the language of energy?"

"There's an intelligence in the tablet. It reads the vibration of all around it."

"Are you saying it knew who you were and allowed you to live?"

"Yes, sir."

"And how did it know you, Miss Valen?"

Dominique knew there was no going back. That awareness gave her the confidence to tell him everything.

"I was part of the group who planted it there."

The president looked at Bruton.

"You believe all this, Charles?"

"I believe what I've heard, so far, sir, yes."

"Say I believe you, Miss Valen," the president said with an edge of doubt. "What did this language of energy say to you?"

Dominique spoke from a knowing far beyond her human intelligence.

"We must be willing to look at and dismantle the denial of our history, and descend into that truth and grapple with it, and take responsibility for the evils we've done."

"You're talking reincarnation and karma."

"I am, sir. What happens in the world is a direct descendant from our lives before."

"And the tablet speaks to a rectification?"

"The tablet identifies the trajectory of our souls, and tracks our incarnations, and in turn allows us the chance to see who we've been and what we've done. And in that knowing we have a chance to unravel those knotted lives and take responsibility for the sum of our actions. And that correction points to a rebalancing of our soul's purpose, the true purpose of why we're here."

"That's quite a task."

"It would be, sir."

And while her nearness to death had imprinted in her a certain courage, a chill invaded her bones.

"Why were you the one the tablet revealed this to?"

"I discovered I was part of the group who placed it in the desert thousands of years ago. But I'm not the only one who can access it."

She was heartened when the president seemed to be taking all this in stride. Perhaps the secrets his position had been privy to through the centuries gave him a context to be open to extreme anomalies.

"Who else is part of this group?"

"The others who survived the warehouse."

"Julian Ledge, Hashim, and Nazir Siraj?"

"Yes, sir."

No one else survived?"

"No, sir."

"You're certain of that?"

"Yes, sir."

"But there are others, who weren't in the warehouse, who are part of this group?"

The president waited for her to continue.

"If you value their safety, Miss Valen, we need to know. ISIS, or whatever the hell they're called now, will not stop until they destroy every one of you, and whoever else they deem may have a connection to the stones and the tablet."

The weight of all she'd unleashed hit her with the force of a firestorm.

"This isn't some expedition, finding artifacts that will some day appear in a museum. One isn't placed in a position as I've been placed, and not made aware of many things best left known to only a few. We've known of the stones for a long time. That tablet has been lore. Until now. You've opened a Pandora's box, Miss Valen."

Dominique's grip on the stone tightened.

"It's ironic," the president continued, "that a discovery meant to save the world puts us in the most danger should that knowledge fall into the wrong hands."

"But the tablet is meant to serve, sir."

"You've missed the point, Miss Valen. It's clear from what you've said that the tablet is a technology for tapping into the trajectory of souls, and using that power to transform history. That power can also be abused."

"But it can only be accessed through absolute love."

"And, what is absolute love? Tell me."

"It's beyond words, sir."

"And if it's not true—that it can only be accessed through this indefinable thing—if it can be manipulated, then what?"

A block of fear seared through her with that possibility.

"It's not a history lesson that's brought us here, Miss Valen. It's a lesson in how to achieve mastery, over ourselves, and each other. Until you, the tablet has been myth. But from what you've told me I believe that's no longer true. And as much as it pains me to say it, I believe Abd al Hashim could be a way out of what looms. And that's why you're here."

She had no idea where this meeting was going, and held tighter to the stone in her hand.

"Hashim knows the collective mind of his people much better than anyone, since he was responsible for shaping it into the Islamic State we know now. Mister Bruton will arrange transport and protection. You'll be able to talk with him in private. We need to know the scope of their operations, beyond what he told Judge Littelton, and we need to know the heart and soul of how they think, in order to be ahead of whatever they plan. For whatever reasons, you've been placed in an invaluable position to shape what's to come. And I trust your commitment to the truth, and our country, will continue to drive you. Dress warm. You'll need it."

The president walked to the door, stopped and turned back.

"Before you leave, you will tell Mister Bruton who the others are."

She knew that was an order.

The president left the room.

Bruton handed Dominique a pad and pen and watched as she wrote down the names of the others.

She handed the pad back to Bruton and said, "I will talk with Hashim. But we will never reach the level of evolution the tablet speaks of until everyone reveals the scope of their operations, and the heart and soul of how they think. That includes all of us."

"It's a good thing you kept that to yourself while he was here. We take this step by step now. It's no longer just your odyssey."

81

Catherine Book flagged a cab down on K Street when her mobile rang. She answered. Dominique told her of meeting with the president and that he'd asked for all the names of those involved for their protection. She asked if Catherine would be willing to use her cottage as a "safe house" for Jhana-Merise, Vincente, Arama, and Nazir.

Catherine was surprised Nazir would be with them.

"Is there a problem with that?" Dominique asked.

"No. Nazir had been staying at the cottage and left. He was afraid of putting me in danger. I didn't want him to go. I'm glad he's okay. I welcome them all. When do you need them there?"

"As soon as possible."

"How's tonight?"

"That'd be great. And you won't mind if a few security guys rotate round the clock for protection? President's orders."

"I understand. Will you be with them?"

"At some point."

"Are you all right?"

"Yes. There's something I need to do."

Catherine saw the cabbie's impatient eyes staring at her in the rearview mirror waiting for her to tell him where she wanted to go. "Virginia Beach," she said.

82

Moonlight made the buildings seem like a series of spooky triangular crop circles.

Dominique shivered looking out the small window of the government prop plane as it descended over the United States super maximum-security unit, known as the Alcatraz of the Rockies.

The plane landed in the middle of nowhere, on ground that shimmered with a skin of white snow. The landscape was set against the silhouette of a mountain range shaped like a hill of elephants.

ADX Florence Prison was in Fremont County, Colorado. The surface of Mars, with cylindrical turrets and razor wire fences, came to her mind as the plane landed. This was a place where dreams of rehabilitation were superseded by the architecture of control. ADX wasn't designed for humanity. It was here Hashim had been brought. And here where Dominique would speak with him. She'd been told by the warden—in a cold delivery that was a perfect match for the arctic freeze of the place—that he was to extend all courtesy to her and that her conversation with Hashim would be private.

A thickset guard carried a folding chair. He led an armed escort of three men to a semi-enclosed "rec-yard" with a series of steel cages. To Dominique it looked like a kennel. The cages were all empty except for the farthest. Hashim stood there, the dim light of a single bulb overhead. Dominique saw Hashim look up as she and her escorts moved across the frozen yard toward him.

Dominique saw in Hashim's razor-sharp posture that he still carried his dignity…in spite of the orange jump suit he wore being too large. A reminder the inmates were small and engulfed by a power greater than themselves, she thought.

The door to the cage screeched across the concrete as the thickset guard opened it. Dominique winced.

"It's music to my ears," Hashim said with a hint of a smile.

The guard opened the chair and placed it inside the cage. "I'll be right over there, ma'am."

He moved to the other end of the area, leaving the cage door opened.

"That's as hospitable as it gets. I'm glad they told you to dress for the weather," he said, looking at the heavy down parka she wore.

"Aren't you cold in just that?"

"You get used to it."

She looked up at the stars through the fenced-in roof. She knew these same seeds of light gazed down at humans across the globe.

"Yes. There's beauty even here. When you have the chance to see it."

He looked up at the stars with her.

"It's surreal landing in this place."

"Try living here."

"They treating you all right?"

"You're here."

"They allowing you to write?"

She could see he wasn't sure what she meant.

"Catherine told me about the poem you gave her. 'There are stories we carry inside...'"

"'...That have slipped beyond the veil of consciousness and wait until a certain time,'" he answered.

The damp chill reached her bones. But it was more than the cold heart of this place. It was for the merciless glaucoma that had dimmed the world, and created the need for places like this—for the cruel world they'd all helped to create.

"Poetry has always been important to me," he said, pulling her from her melancholy. "No one seems interested in exploring that."

"A window to the soul?"

"Nobody's born wanting to kill. It's incremental."

"So, lead with culture? Is that what you're saying?"

"It has strategic value—empathy."

She moved in close to him and whispered, "I need a way into your thinking. Their thinking."

"I figured that's why they sent you. Others have found the tablet, haven't they?"

"They know the area where it is, but haven't gotten to it. Special Forces killed the first wave that came to the warehouse. The second wave died in a sandstorm."

"There will be others."

"We know."

Hashim took a step out of the cage.

"Five feet, no more," the guard ordered.

Hashim waved his hand in acknowledgment. He turned back to Dominique.

"How we live is important to getting a deeper understanding of our thinking. There was no speech of bin Laden's in which he didn't recite poetry."

"I know. And the raid in Abbottabad found books by Bob Woodward and Noam Chomsky."

"His cabinet of curiosities. No one is looking at the fact Zarqawi wept. And Muhammad Omar acted on dreams. But Ahlam al-Nasr. She's who you need to study now. She's the poet of jihad."

"I'm not here about poetry."

"You're here to learn how we think. The key is in our tears, our dreams, and our words."

She realized she'd gotten caught in her drive to make sense of the mystery and the search, when a pivotal answer was in the deeper truth of what he said.

"The president listened to you?"

"Yes. Even the parts I wouldn't be surprised if he thought me mad to say."

"But he didn't think you mad, did he?"

"It didn't seem that way. Tears, dreams, and poetry may be a harder sell."

"Are you familiar with the magazine, *Dabiq*?"

"No."

"It's a glossy ISIS periodical that focuses on issues of unity, truth-seeking, community, and jihad."

"Sounds lovely."

"It portrays the Islamic State as they see themselves, as I used to see it. Boasting victories and painting romantic images of the restoration of an Islamic golden age, and heralding a new caliphate based on holy war."

"Charming."

"Dabiq is also a town in Syria. It's supposed to be the location for one of the final battles according to Muslim myth."

"The apocalypse?"

"Yes. One of the magazine's monthly issues was called 'Just Terror.' That's who you'll be dealing with—in case you forgot—when you attempt to tell them we share a spiritual DNA that the tablet speaks of."

"Can you help me?"

"I can't give you a lesson plan on how to transform the way we've been taught to think."

"What can you do?"

"Whatever there is, if anything, I don't want to go back to that dark place inside. And, even if it were possible, I couldn't do it from here."

"From where could you do it?"

"I'd have to be in the heart of it again. And I'd be killed the moment they knew I was there."

"Not if they believed your surrender was a ruse."

Hashim chuckled.

"You have an active imagination, Miss Valen. You expect too much. No one would believe me."

"But if they did?"

"I don't imagine your Secret Service would relish the idea of setting up all that deception for me. Is this why your president sent you? To turn me into your spy?"

"He sent me to ask for your help. How that might be accomplished was never discussed."

She remembered before all this, before the warehouse, when she was sitting in that Mosul bar, wanting, hoping one day to be able to plumb the depths of Hashim's mind, to put him in her journalist's crosshairs, to know what made him tick—to find a way into him and his culture, and extract a grain of their essence that might give her a way to shift their drive from blood and vengeance to healing. Perhaps that she'd been unable to extract a grain of reconciliation from her own countrymen fueled her passion to find it in the enemy. She'd been looking for a way through that wall a long time.

"The tablet isn't magic, Miss Valen. There is no magic there."

"I know. But it is a road map."

She watched Hashim compute the complications in the plan she'd set before him.

"Is Nazir still in America?"

"Yes. Why?"

"You would need to send him in first, since, as far as I can tell, he hasn't been tainted by my actions. He'd need to see what chance I have to influence anyone still in power. That is, if they were to believe there was no surrender, and if you could get me out of here."

"You think he'd do that?"

"You would need to be the one to ask him. You do know this is a long shot."

"If we don't try, we'll continue to pick each other off the minute anyone gets close to the tablet."

"Yes. For all its power, it can still unleash the worst in us."

"*Evil is the greatest source of transformation.*"

"Where did you hear that?"

"In the energy of the tablet."

"And you're telling me this, why?"

"I believe you are our *source* for that transformation."

"Because of the evil I've done."

"Yes."

"You believe I have control over which way ISIS goes?"

"I have to believe it. Otherwise, why are we here? Why have we been brought together?"

He reached out and held her hand.

Her mind said to pull away, yet instinct kept her from moving.

Prisoners weren't allowed to touch anyone, but Hashim had blocked the guard's view.

This was the first time they'd touched since the warehouse, when they'd held hands and stopped the ground from opening under them. Her hope was that they could stop the ground from swallowing up the world. But she was afraid.

"How do you expect a culture to change when you still fear me?"

She locked in on him and held tighter to his hand, as if the complexities that lingered might evaporate in the intimacy.

"You must erase those traces of fear still clenched to your DNA before you ask anyone else to do the same. It will not be easy. It will be impossible. Because beheadings aren't something jihadists cherry-pick from medieval tradition. They're at the heart of that tradition. I will do what I can to help you change that, even if it means my life... which I know it will."

83

Tuesday, October 13

Dawn streamed in through the blinds. Jhana-Merise opened her eyes. She got out of bed in one of the guest rooms of the cottage. She went into the kitchen. Vincente looked up at her and said, "We can't keep imposing on these kind people."

"We need to be here, Father."

With anyone else that answer would be presumptuous. But he knew his daughter's humility was the source of her zeal.

Vincente's mind weighed with the fact they'd been in America almost three weeks, much longer than he'd anticipated. And it terrified him they would fail in the mission to help bring enemies together, and Jhana-Merise, and they all would be harmed.

Vincente believed more in God of late. It was a different God. Not the God of his youth taught by priests and nuns. Not the God of the church. He believed there was a greater power not resting in one place—like air, invisible, but sustaining life. This was the power his daughter had grasped. A power she offered him in the form of her life force and passion. But he was scared. Scared for all of them who'd been brought together. Yet he knew he was here to protect them, even in the doubt and concern that lingered. The extent of that protection was unknown. He'd been there for his daughter. Could he be there for the others? He looked at her with tired and worried eyes, unable and unwilling to keep his unease from her.

Nazir entered the kitchen. He was surprised to see Vincente and Jhana-Merise up so early.

"Sorry. I didn't mean to—"

"It's all right," Vincente said.

Jhana-Merise took Nazir's hand and led him to a corner of the room.

"You're going to have to go back to Iraq," she said.

"Why?"

"To lay groundwork there. In the land of our ancestors."

Jhana-Merise told him about the land of Sumer in the southern region of Mesopotamia, which is modern-day Iraq and Kuwait. It was the cradle of civilization.

"The first settlers were not Sumerians, but a people of unknown origin, from a prehistoric period in this region archaeologists have termed the Ubaid, which is said to mean, 'servant of Allah'. We were those people. We are those people. And we must return to that land."

She looked at him like a mother whose heart held all the love in the world. "But first, there is work to be done here."

Vincente looked at the two of them and knew she was no longer his daughter. She belonged to the world. He'd always suspected that, and in his way lived to protect her so that she might do this work.

"Don't be sad, Father. We are all part of each other. Always have and always will be."

The energy in the kitchen changed as the scent of roses drifted in.

Ancient drawings appeared on the walls of the room. Cave paintings from long ago.

They stared at the story that unfolded.

A series of primitive figures rising from sleep—floating in a smokeless fire.

"We've been asleep a long time," Jhana-Merise said. "We're awakening now."

PART EIGHT

Guardians

84

Friday, October 16

Nazir entered the Islamic Mosque and Cultural Center in D.C. as the evening call to prayer sounded. Dominique had told him of the meeting she had with Hashim, and for there to be any chance of Hashim finding his way back into their world, Nazir would be the one to test the waters. It would be a risk. A risk because it would be based on a scenario created by the FBI and CIA to perpetrate the lie that Hashim had never surrendered but was captured and had escaped. That's why he was in hiding. And that's why he needed to get word out that he wasn't a traitor.

That the leaders of the mujahideen would believe this was a long shot, but the endless war on terror needed long shots, and Dominique believed it could be done. She had convinced Bruton and the president, each who'd realized, that since what had happened in the warehouse, there were forces at work to help them accomplish an unprecedented act.

Nazir's body thrummed with the rush of possibility and the chanting that reverberated in the large room that rivaled cathedrals. He was pulled to pray with the men gathered on intricately woven rugs in vibrant colors, for they reminded him of home. But he didn't pray.

He moved respectfully through the halls down the main stairs to a corridor and series of classrooms.

At the end of one corridor a door had been left opened, and coming from inside—a familiar voice. He edged his way close to the opened door, and for a while, listened as Mariam Sarif spoke in Arabic teaching the Qur'an to a group of young children.

One of the boys in the back row turned and saw Nazir, who motioned for him to turn his attention back to the teacher. But the boy smiled and didn't shift his focus from the stranger in the doorway.

A few of the other students caught wind of the boy's distraction and they, too, turned their attention to Nazir, who then saw their attention whip back to the front of the room, and watched as their eyes followed Mariam to the back door.

She wore a hijab, and gasped when she saw Nazir had distracted the students.

The students at recess, Mariam and Nazir stood in the back of the empty classroom.

"Where have you been?" she asked.

"Hiding."

"Did you hear about the raid on the dry cleaners?"

"Yes. And your father's death. I'm sorry."

He touched her cheek.

She blushed in the unexpected intimacy and stepped back.

"How did they find him?"

"I don't know." But it was a lie. He knew Hashim told the FBI about the farmhouse in Pennsylvania.

She looked out the window at her students playing in the courtyard. He stood beside her, and could see in her tears that now she felt more alone than ever.

She had told him the night they'd met that her mother had been collateral damage from a U.S. Forces air raid when Mariam was young. And he knew her father, Sayyid, was her one connection to family and tradition. He also knew she'd had a sheltered youth, and he'd come closest to her feeling of belonging. He knew his presence brought that longing back.

He wanted to tell her the truth of why he was here. He wanted to tell her about the experience in the desert, about what had happened to him and Hashim since, but needed her to believe he was still who he had been. So he stayed silent. Maybe, at some point, he could speak the truth. But not now.

He looked at her with love and sadness. Love for the life they might have had, sadness for the lies he still had to tell.

"Can you get me a meeting with Pashtar?" he asked.

"Yes," she answered. "But why?"

"It's best you don't know that right now."

He took her hand. It was damp and trembling. He knew his coming back would break her heart.

85

The club was packed and loud when Nazir met with Pashtar Abbas. Pashtar was in his forties, and in spite of—or maybe because of—his large, brooding frame, he was attractive to both the men and women who clustered around his corner table in the club. More likely, it was because he was rich and powerful. These were things he would never be under the Islamic State. But here, Pashtar had made himself a conduit into an underground world, and access to terrorist cells.

In the room full of partiers, Nazir caught Pashtar's attention.

He also saw a young man being quietly escorted out of the club in a chokehold.

The back room of the club was quiet. Soundproofing provided isolation from the noise on the other side of the walls. Nazir also sensed the isolation kept what noise happened in here from reaching other ears.

"*As-salamu alaykum,*" Pashtar said as he eyed Nazir. His words were clipped, like shots.

"*Wa-Alaikum-Salaam,*" Nazir responded.

Pashtar embraced him.

"Welcome," he said and motioned for Nazir to sit in one of the expensive leather chairs.

"Something to drink, Nazir?"

Nazir shook his head.

"You don't mind if I do?"

Nazir shook his head again.

Pashtar plopped ice into a tumbler and poured himself a healthy shot of vodka.

"This doesn't offend you, does it?"

Nazir just looked at him.

"Good," Pashtar said as he plopped into one of the chairs.

There was puffiness about Pashtar's face, and also stone-cold hardness. His eyes were dark orbs—not what eyes should be—mirrors that reflected light out from the soul. There was no light reflected here. It reminded Nazir of his teachers before Hashim. Their dark, impenetrable gaze compelled attention and instilled fear. That training Nazir knew would hold him in good stead as he maneuvered through these treacherous waters.

"Mariam tells me you want to talk with the imam," Pashtar said, staring at him.

"Yes."

"You may be able to persuade a young, vulnerable woman with your youth and charm," Pashtar's words were ominous "but with Hashim's surrender and your connection to him, why should I trust you at all?"

"Because there was no surrender."

"What do you mean?"

"It was a ploy by the FBI."

"And how do you know this?"

"I know where Hashim is hiding."

"Hiding?"

"Yes. He knows you all believe he was a traitor. That's what they want you to believe."

"Why?"

"There's already a fatwa on him. His own people will do what the CIA and FBI never could. That's their plan."

Nazir waited, calm in the deadly consequence of this falling on deaf ears.

Pashtar slammed his drink on the table next to him and pushed his large body out of the chair.

"Who else knows of this?"

"You're the first."

"And to what do I owe the honor?"

"I need your help. I'm placing my life in your hands. It's your trust I need before I can let anyone else know."

Pashtar's need for acknowledgment and inclusion was common knowledge among the cells. It was the one thing that gave Nazir hope. He also knew that if he could get past this test there would be a chance he could succeed with the imam.

"So, his surrender was a lie?"

"Yes. He was captured. And escaped. The rest is the lie."

Nazir's heart pumped in the absence of a response.

Pashtar's laughter filled the room.

The silence that followed was deadly.

"How do I know I can trust you, and this story?"

"Test me."

Pashtar smiled. Arms at his side. He had the attitude of a gunslinger about to duel. His eyes fixed on Nazir, who knew Pashtar could kill him in an instant.

Pashtar took out a mobile from his pants pocket and made a call that was answered on the first ring.

"Bring him around back," Pashtar said, and ended the call.

He opened a drawer in the table next to him, and pulled out a switchblade.

Nazir stiffened.

Pashtar put a hand on Nazir's shoulder. His dark eyes, piercing.

"Follow me."

Pashtar and Nazir waited in the narrow back alley of the club.

A black sedan pulled into the alley.

A Caucasian man in a sharp, dark suit got out of the sedan.

Banging came from the trunk of the car.

Nazir was on high alert.

Pashtar popped open the trunk.

Inside, the young man who'd been dragged from the club was tied and gagged.

Nazir looked at Pashtar.

"You asked for a test. Allah gives to those who ask, and are ready."

He handed Nazi the switchblade, and pointed to the young man in the trunk.

"Who is he?" Nazir asked.

"Someone who lied."

The young man's eyes opened wide. He kicked his feet against the inside of the trunk.

His gagged pleas were cut short when Pashtar grabbed the young man's throat, and cold-cocked him with his other hand.

"Now, kill him," Pashtar said.

Hesitation meant death.

Nazir steeled himself, flicked open the switchblade, and slit the young man's throat.

The three men watched him die.

The man in the suit slammed the lid of the trunk shut, got back into the car, and took off down the alley.

Nazir stood there, bloodied knife in his hand. His heart raced.

Pashtar took the knife.

"You'll be contacted," he said and went back into the club.

Pounding bass from the club's music bled into Nazir's ears.

After he'd killed Taliq, the FBI undercover agent, Nazir thought he'd shook off the compulsion to kill, but now he realized how deep the bloodlust from his jihadist life had burrowed into him. He'd fooled himself into believing he'd changed.

The stranger he killed may have been an innocent man. But innocent or guilty it placed Nazir back into the world he'd left behind. This test reminded him of what he was still capable. It was a proficiency he knew would keep him alive. A double-edged sword he had to embrace.

In the journey to healing there would be more bloodshed.

86

Sunday, October 18

It was late Sunday night in the empty restaurant in a strip mall on the edge of D.C.

Pashtar led Nazir to a thin man with a white beard, wearing a gray suit, and sitting at a table.

The imam's face was in shadow. And even in shadow, or because of it, Nazir sensed a powerful energy.

He had the charisma of a mystic in a suit. And from experience, Nazir knew that magnetism would turn lethal if he didn't convince him Hashim had never given himself up. He needed the imam to believe.

Nazir knew suicide bombers back in Mosul. Young men who'd offered themselves to jihad. They rarely talked of their fear, they'd been so indoctrinated into the cause and reward there was little space in their fevered brains for fear. But the ones who managed to be honest, even if for a moment, spoke of their doubt, questioning the reasons for the vests they wore. Questioning the truth of the virgins that waited as reward. But they couldn't let that deter them from the job at hand. Families depended on their choice. Poverty, hopelessness, and coercion were the coins of this realm. That certain fear crept up Nazir's legs as he steadied himself, standing across from this man, this stranger—one of his own people, at least until what had happened in the desert changed his purpose. But it didn't mitigate him feeling like those young men, for the vest he wore now was deception, and would mean death if he failed to convince the imam he was still on their side.

The imam motioned for Nazir to sit across from him.

Pashtar moved back, giving the men privacy.

Nazir's lie began.

He told the imam that Hashim was in hiding somewhere far from here. The information about Sayyid Sarif at the farmhouse had come from the undercover agent, Taliq—whom Nazir had killed—not from Hashim as had been rumored.

The imam pressed for details of what happened.

Nazir spun the lie that Hashim had been captured, and after the trial escaped with the help of someone from a renegade cell who had been embedded within the FBI, and was killed protecting him. The FBI and CIA were willing to look like fools in Hashim's escape, because they realized they could use what had happened, and spin a scenario that Hashim had surrendered, and that would create chaos within all the cells, who would believe he was a traitor. They banked on a fatwa to take him out, when they couldn't. That's why Hashim was in hiding.

"It was a deception?" the imam said, his voice filled with doubt.

"Yes," Nazir answered, his voice composed and self-assured.

"And how do you know this?"

"From the one who died protecting Hashim."

The answer came as if it were the truth—it came from another source—the same source that allowed him to remain calm, as he saw the imam calculating what he had laid out.

Nazir waited for the imam to make the next move. It would be with more questions or his death.

In the space of this keen awareness, Nazir's body pulsated—and the air around him filled with the scent of roses. Did the imam, and Pashtar, smell the fragrance, too? He couldn't tell. He embraced the disquiet and the question as he sensed Pashtar's body tense in the corner of the room.

The imam's face was expressionless. He rubbed his thumb over the crease in the paper napkin on the table.

Nazir watched as the imam took a breath deeper than before.

"It was brave, your coming here."

In the silence that followed, Nazir held his own against the authority that had come to hear him.

"We need you to do something for us, Nazir."

Nazir opened his arms in a gesture of accepting whatever that might be.

"There are many young people in America whose hearts are attached to ours. Their loyalty must be cultivated. We believe you are the one to help do that. We believe Allah has brought you to us for that purpose."

The imam raised his hand as if summoning. And from the kitchen Mariam brought in a tray of tea and sweets and served the two men.

The imam took Nazir's hand, then Mariam's, brought them together and said, "She will be your conduit to the young ones whom you will teach to serve."

Was the bringing of their hands together a marriage to the cause, or something else? There were multiple levels at play. Was the imam aware of Nazir's new allegiance? Was this a trap to discern his loyalty?

Nazir remained in the questions, as the scent of roses swirled. A scent no one else seemed to notice.

"What about Hashim?" Nazir asked, sensing the imam still had questions.

For the first time in the meeting, the imam smiled.

"Yes. We will meet. But first, we need you to begin teaching Mariam's young ones. And we know you will do it with much discretion."

Nazir felt another purpose within the imam's order, and knew this was another level to gain his trust. He would need to stay in the skin of his former self to survive.

It was another test. Allah gives to those who ask and are ready.

Yet, as he watched the imam breathe in the air around him, he believed he smelled the roses, too. And maybe, his charge to teach the young ones had a purpose closer to his own.

87

Monday, October 19

Nazir stood in front of Mariam's class in the Islamic Mosque and Cultural Center. The boys who had been distracted by him standing in the hallway a few days before sat in rapt attention as he spoke of the Qur'an. But as the words came out his memory was in another place and time, for he saw himself in the young boys leaning into his authority.

He'd thought much about the meeting with the imam, and made the choice to go with what he believed—that the imam had smelled the roses, too. He was gambling with his life.

Nazir wouldn't recruit and inspire these children as he had been taught. And, now that he was in the position of doing just that, he had no idea what role to play. It was one thing to believe in something, another to put it into practice, when the implementation could cost his life. How could he, on one level, seem to teach jihad...yet on another, get into their young minds and shift them out of wanting to become suicide bombers? What if his reading of the imam was wrong? It was a paradox for which he had no answer, and it terrified him.

War was clear. Dead. Alive. His circumstance now was a grey zone, and he thought of his grandmother, who'd tried to teach him about the complexities of life, but he'd refused to listen. She was the woman who'd cared for him after his parents were killed. The woman who said he was spared for a reason. Who said he could never bring his parents back with blood. That blood for blood was not God's way. She'd never stopped trying to impart the futility of war or relinquish her vow to infuse in him the love of all men, which she believed Allah spoke.

He cried, for he saw the disrespect he'd given her even though he'd loved her. And he let himself cry, for he knew Mariam and the young boys would believe his tears were for the beauty of the Qur'an. And he let the lie linger. He knew what was needed must be done with lies and "much discretion."

Mariam said to the class, "You should all be so moved by the words of the great Prophet like Mister Siraj."

Nazir nodded and smiled through his tears.

As he told the students of his life in Mosul, a woman came to the door of the classroom and motioned to Mariam, who went to her.

The woman whispered something to Mariam, who turned to Nazir and said, "There are a few things I need to attend to."

She turned to the class, directed them to be good and attentive to their guest, and left.

Nazir wiped his tears. He went to the door and closed it. If he was ever going to attempt to cultivate the seed of non-violence, now was the time. Now was the test he believed the imam had set before him. The test he was betting his life on.

He walked among the boys, shifted from his life in Mosul, and told them a tale he called, "The Mystery in the Desert."

He hadn't planned to tell them about what had happened to him, but realized he was being guided and trusted the scent of roses, of which he could see only he was aware.

He told the story of how fierce enemies had an experience they couldn't explain when a ball of fire exploded in the desert and left them alive. It set each of them on a path to find the source of the fire from the sky, and the mystery of its effect on them that had changed their hearts. And they went in search of each other—in search of an answer that would bring them, and many others back together, from a long ago time.

The boys leaned in. Nazir knew the power of story. He knew the power of lies and how they could persuade. He knew the power of truth and how it resonated with the heart. He also knew the power of mystery and how that could capture and hold attention. How to serve all these and not get killed was the dangerous undertaking before him.

He thought of what Jhana-Merise had told him, about the awakening of a spiritual DNA. It gave him an idea to plant in the story he was telling. And he spoke of a young girl from a land far away who awoke one day with the knowledge of how to bring these once enemies together. She knew it was Allah who'd brought the fire to the desert. Fire that would burn the hate. But it was a quiet fire, lit from inside these strangers that would lead them to what Allah called The Greater Jihad. The jihad of love.

Nazir's grandmother's voice coursed through him, and he said aloud, "Blood for blood is not God's way."

The boys' attention turned to the back of the room. And Nazir saw Mariam standing in the doorway.

Class was over. The boys were gone. Mariam confronted Nazir about what he'd been teaching. "Blood for blood is not God's way?"

"We need to open their hearts before we can fill it with jihad," Nazir replied.

"Is that what Hashim taught you?"

"Yes. Hashim said, 'when the heart is open Allah will find a place.'"

He was telling her the truth, but for him the place Allah would find was love, not one of blood.

He wondered if the questioning look in her eyes held a seed for her transformation out of the violence, or maybe it was a look that questioned his loyalty. He couldn't tell. But he needed to address it. And to do that he told her about his life, in hopes his passage to jihad would quell whatever doubts of his loyalty might be lingering in her mind. Doubts she might not be aware of, but which could rise and be used against him. He knew gossip could be a plague. Lies were his salvation in this.

"My grandmother called me *Shaheed*," he said.

"Martyr. She wanted you to be a martyr?"

"Yes," he said lying, silently asking his grandmother for forgiveness for using her this way.

He could see Mariam was caught off-guard.

And, the more details he related of men in suicide vests, the more she shuddered at the savage reality of those actions. He'd heard her father speak of the glory of sacrifice, and had seen its effect on her, for he knew how much she admired him.

Nazir spoke of sacrifice, too. But he spoke of the blood in a way he knew she hadn't been exposed.

He told her of one martyr who never made it to heaven, never got the virgins, even though the blast from his bomb was strong enough to kill twenty infidels.

"He wasn't a hero because he didn't die. Neither charred eyes, nor a face like bubbled tar pleased Allah."

It was a gamble speaking this graphic, but he wanted the gruesome details of jihad to burrow inside her. Because he believed horror this raw could move her. He needed it to move her at a place inside, a place in which he hoped an ember of The Greater Jihad burned.

88

Rain beat heavily against the windows of Bruton's office. Dominique saw turmoil in the man she'd come to respect, for she knew how much he had at stake, too.

"It's important to look to the future of what's been presented," Bruton said. "But present dangers are not to be taken lightly. Is the relationship with the young Sarif woman going to be an asset or liability?"

"You mean, is there a romance that could thwart or support Nazir's purpose?"

"Do you have a sense of which it might be?"

"No, I don't. And I'm not putting him in any more danger, pushing him one way or the other with her."

"His life was in danger the minute he landed here. Do you think he can change their hearts without anyone noticing?"

Maybe the world couldn't change. Maybe darkness would always rage against the light. Could Nazir change hearts without anyone noticing? It was a good question, and one she'd suppressed because she didn't want to believe it might be true. But Dominique also believed what Jhana-Merise had said about the reawakening of their souls, and saw how that could ignite a quiet fire of love from inside. It was a worthy pursuit. A narrative that told her she'd been asleep all these years, even running through the clusterfuck of firefights.

"I know you're frightened, Charles. I am, too. But we have a chance to do something that can change us—maybe even change the world."

"And you plan to let Nazir go deeper into the lion's den to find that out? Who's putting him in more danger now?"

"He's not going to do it alone from here on."

"What do you mean?"

"He's going to introduce me to Mariam. She's our conduit to Pashtar, and to the imam."

"If you think that isn't a death sentence, you're more naive than I thought."

"I was with Nazir and Hashim in the warehouse. I have information the imam will want to know. I'll tell him I've been in contact with Hashim ever since he set foot here. All of which is true."

"And what if he decides you're not worth the risk?"

"We've known all our lives that we're more than we know. We can break free of the tribal beliefs handed down to us by fear. What we've been thrust into is mystical in design. But it doesn't make it any less valid than the air we breathe, which we can't see either but is measurable. This is measurable, too. I believe the imam will listen."

Bruton touched her shoulder in a gesture of friendship. "And where is Julian in all this?"

"Making his way to a truth that has eluded him."

89

Julian stood at the door to the Victorian era master bedroom his parents once shared. The housekeeper had kept the ornate curtains and damask bed sheets pristine, as if the appearance of cleanliness and order reflected reality. It didn't.

The senator made his way up the main staircase to the master suites. He saw his son staring into the bedroom.

"Your mother said you were here. You can go in, it won't bite."

"You visited Jack Dean," Julian said. "Did he know you'd had the same chance at all this that I have?"

"Yes. There was a time when we shared our lives."

"I'd always wondered what it was that had terrified you when I was a boy. It terrified Mother, too. I understand that now."

He walked into the bedroom.

"I remember coming in here when I was young. There weren't many of those days, but there was love here once."

Ledge stood at the threshold to the room.

"When I was in the catacombs," Julian said, "I could feel you there with me. You had a longing for something out of reach."

He faced his father. It'd been a long time since he had compassion for him.

"You had an experience like I did, and you turned away."

The anguish Julian felt in the catacombs he saw now in his father's eyes.

"There were others," Ledge said.

"Who were they?"

"I don't know."

"Not Jack Dean?"

"He had the information, but that was all. He was a messenger."

"Whose career you and Bruton killed."

Julian felt the thrum of pain that emanated from his father.

"I've turned away from much, too."

"But not this," Ledge said.

"No. As much as I struggle with it, not this."

Julian turned toward the door and saw his mother standing there. She didn't have a drink in her hand.

"I see you found each other," she said.

"Maybe," Julian answered. "Maybe we'll all find each other again."

90

Wednesday, October 21

To avoid the chance of Mariam making any connection to the journalist in the warehouse bombing, Nazir introduced her to Dominique, under a fictitious name. They were at the mosque where Mariam worked.

Dominique, wearing a dark hijab, could see Mariam trusted Nazir in the way she listened and accepted what he told her about how he and his visitor came to be connected and committed to jihad.

Something happened to Dominique as she stood in the hallway of the mosque. She was being downloaded with this young woman's history.

Slipping into the skin of Mariam's life—her sorrow for not knowing her mother—her feelings of being "the other" in America—the longing to be part of the culture of her father, which included his passion for justice through jihad. And her feelings for Nazir complicated an already perilous situation.

Dominique had spent years wanting to get into the mindset of the mujahideen, to understand them and change the course of the violence. That way broke open in her conversation with Hashim at ADX prison. And now she was making contact with Mariam's soul.

From what Nazir had told Dominique of Mariam, she knew this young woman didn't fall into the usual grievances that gave rise to terrorism in the name of God. She'd been neither alienated, humiliated, nor dispossessed in the ways that drove men and women to sacrifice themselves. Yes, she'd been guided by her father's grievances, but Dominique could see beneath Mariam's anger—a force of which Mariam wasn't even aware was tempering her fervor. And so, Dominique talked with her about the prophets and poets that inspired their cause.

Dominique's meeting with Hashim in prison gave her much insight.

She'd spent time learning of the work and life of the woman he'd spoken of—the "poetess of the Islamic State." And when she mentioned Ahlam al-Nasr to Mariam, she lit up, as if encountering a kindred spirit.

The authority of verse had no rival in Arabic culture. That was what Hashim wanted to impress upon Dominique. Desert nomads composed their earliest poems. And while the Qur'an had harsh words for these troubadours, these men and women of words had become companions of Muhammad, praising him in life and elegizing him in death.

Mariam talked of al-Nasr's book of verse, *The Blaze of Truth*, which consisted of a hundred and seven poems in Arabic—elegies to mujahideen, laments for prisoners, and victory odes.

Mariam was well informed of this history. She talked of when in the spring of 2011, and protests in Syria broke out against the rule of Bashar al-Assad, how al-Nasr took the side of the demonstrators. The poems she wrote stood as witness to the regime's violent crackdown, and she was radicalized by what she saw.

Mariam spoke of a verse al-Nasr wrote in reaction to that spring—of shattered brains. Bones cracked. Throats drilled. Scattered limbs. And blood that ran through the streets.

Dominique saw her own fervor had reached deep into Mariam's, as Mariam's fervor was reaching into her. Their souls connected. It was unsettling and beautiful.

She could see Nazir felt it, too.

91

Dominique hadn't been in Adrien Kurt's therapy office since she'd come back from her experience in the catacombs. She appreciated that he was willing to stay late to see her on short notice, because she needed to be here. She didn't know how to process all of what had happened to her in the mosque.

"Every bone in my body tells me not to go any further with this."

"That's the remnant of your fear," Kurt said. "You've overpowered it for so long you never gave it the chance to rise up so you could choose it, and dismantle it. You've wanted to turn jihad around a long time. And from what you've told me, you have a grasp on a lot of it now—from the download of Mariam's life—to the engagement around the poet. That's a rare combination. And a serious confrontation to the terror you're feeling. It isn't going to let go until you choose to let it go."

She noticed a beautiful white porcelain figurine on his desk.

"That's new," she said, pointing to it. She needed a distraction.

"Yes. She's called, Quan Yin. She's a Buddhist bodhisattva. She represents compassion and mercy."

"May I…"

"Sure."

Dominique went to the desk and held the figurine.

"You've been guided to the place where you are, Dominique."

"Divine intervention?" she said with a nervous chuckle.

"What do you call putting on the mind of another?"

"So, you're not going to try and talk me out of it?"

"You're not afraid of what happened. You're terrified you'll succeed. Besides, there are forces seen and unseen that want you to succeed."

"And forces that don't."

"There are."

She placed the Quan Yin back on the desk, but couldn't leave her presence.

Dominique had lived with forces that didn't want her to succeed all her life. Being a woman was part of that equation. Being successful, the other.

She spoke of the last time she and Kurt met here, after she'd returned from the desert, and how Kurt had said he understood what she went through.

"You never told me all of what you understood."

"You weren't ready to hear it."

"Am I now?"

"I believe you are."

He told her he was in the desert a long time ago, in the same catacombs where she and Julian were led.

"How long ago?"

"Long enough."

"I'm listening."

"I was one of a group who came to find a location to hide the stones in order that those who followed might be led to the tablet."

"Are we having this conversation?"

"You asked. What do you think you've been being exposed to since that hospital room in Pittsburgh?"

The memories of her almost dying as a child, and the near escapes from death, moored her to a deeper perception of the path she'd been on.

"Were you responsible for the missile going off course?"

"I was part of the energy that made that happen."

She didn't know anything about him. She'd avoided knowing anything about him.

"Who are you?" she cried.

"I know you want answers to all the questions you have. But anything I say, beyond what I've said, your mind will argue with. So, why don't you accept that I'm here to help you. I've always been here to help you."

"Can you help us survive what we're attempting to do?"

"We already are. But there's no guarantee. We're not God. We're guides."

"What about Mariam?"

"There are memories that will open for her. And you must be there to help her understand."

"And Julian?"

"He'll make sure the others are safe."

"Others?"

"Those who've been brought together at the cottage. There are many of us who've been waiting for this. Waiting to help shift the downward spiral of the world. And, because of you, it has begun."

92

Sunday, October 25

Dominique sat across from the imam in the same empty restaurant in the strip mall on the edge of D.C. where Nazir first met him the previous Sunday. She'd been here a few minutes, but time had slowed, and each second seemed elastic.

It was within that yielding space that she knew him.

Not from this life, but something deep in the past. It was a web from another level of another reality, the doors of which continued to open in inimitable ways.

If there was a center to her experience of him it was his eyes. They were ice-blue. An odd color for someone from his culture. Also, beautiful and frightening. She'd seen eyes like that before.

Pashtar, again, lurked in the shadows.

"We are the children of a ravaged, despised people, fighting with whatever means we can to recover our dignity. Nothing more, nothing less." The imam addressed Dominique with respect. "Our homeland is violated. We spend the evenings gathering our dead and the mornings burying them. And you are comfortable in your refuge here while an inferno consumes us in another part of the world."

He leaned into her.

"I know about your brother, Miss Valen. We've each lost loved ones. How is your rage at his death different than ours with the young men and boys who come back to us dead from your bullets and bombs?"

"It's not different."

"You're an eminent journalist trying to understand. I appreciate that. But there is nothing for you here."

He rose to leave.

"I think there might be," she said.

He stopped. His eyes on her.

"If you bring the truth."

She'd been looking for the truth a long time, and knew he was part of it now. But how could she speak truth to him with lies?

She knew she couldn't.

"You're right. Maybe there is nothing for me here," she said.

She rose to leave.

"Maybe there is," he said.

She stopped. And wondered if he was being guided, too.

"You have protected Nazir, and he has told me of how you harbored Hashim. Thank you, for that."

She knew whatever holy space had opened was about to disappear if she didn't act. Even if it were a lie.

"Hashim is in hiding because he fears for his life, because of what you believe he did. And because our government is looking for him, too."

"It's hard not to believe he surrendered and revealed things with all the press it captured."

"That was meant to send chaos through your cause. We already had information about the dry cleaner cell and the farmhouse."

She knew her story must line up with what Nazir had told him. And the greater truth in what she'd come to accomplish through these lies gave her the certitude to continue.

The imam's eyes had the ability to terrify even as they drew her in. It was a charisma she'd experienced in few leaders. The ones that had it radiated energy hard to resist.

An electric current ran through her, and adrenaline pumped in the face of this life force.

"Set up the meeting with Hashim, Miss Valen."

She knew the feeling of having a heightened perceptive power and reckless daring from being in the middle of war zones, she also was acutely aware that she had placed herself closer to a roadside bomb being here. She trusted the empathy she saw in the imam's ice-blue eyes was the truth.

93

Dominique and Kurt listened to the harsh wind thrumming at the windows of his office.

She read from a dog-eared copy of a book she held in her hands.

"'We're given a choice every day to go through doors and remember who we are. If we choose to avoid it, life will go on. We may even find bravery with which to confront what comes our way. But we will be blind to what we choose to not see.'"

"Prophetic for what you're going through."

"I was seeing it as encouraging. Your take has an ominous ring to it."

"It doesn't need to."

She put the book down.

"Okay. Your turn," she said.

"So. The imam has ice-blue eyes."

"Yes."

"That's rare in his culture. Imam Mālik had blue eyes."

"Who?"

"He was born and lived in Medina in the eighth century. He supported the Sunni doctrine of beatific vision."

"Belief in the afterlife."

"You're up on your Sunni doctrine."

"How do you know about Mālik?"

"Stay long enough in war, you grow antennae for history, and the invisible."

"Is that what this is? Centuries worth of antennae?"

"If you believe you and the imam share a past, use your antennae to find out what that is."

"You can't tell me?"

"No."

"I thought that's what you do."

"It's not. If there's a past with the imam, you need to go deep inside yourself to find it."

Dominique looked around the room. There was a scent permeating the space. A scent with which she was familiar.

"Where's that smell coming from?" she asked.

"What smell?"

"Blood. It's blood."

"Can you taste it?"

She ran her tongue over the inside of her mouth. The taste of bitter iron traveled up the back of her throat.

"What's happening?"

"It's another door opening."

"How many doors are there?"

"As many as needed."

"I guess your ominous take was closer than mine."

He guided her to the chair.

She sat.

"Close your eyes. Whatever happens, you're safe. I'm here."

The taste of blood was stronger in her mouth.

The dark behind her lids exposed a place.

Her left hand reached out as if feeling for something. She had a quick intake of breath.

"What's happening?"

"There's blood on the walls."

"Where are you?"

"A hospital, I think."

"What can you see?"

"There's scattered medical supplies, syringes, bloodied bandages on the floor. The floor and walls are ravaged by bullets."

"Is anyone there?"

"I don't see anyone. It's quiet."

"Is there a window you can look out? A door you can walk through?"

"There's a window."

"Walk to it, tell me what you see."

Kurt watched as Dominique's feet pulsed into the rug on the floor of his office, like a cat pawing a carpet. It was as if she were moving, gripping the ground, but she remained seated.

"Are you at the window?"

"Yes."

"What's out there?"

She had another quick intake of breath.

"There's an old man. And a young boy with him. They're watching me. They're in a park."

"What do you mean a park?"

"It's a park, a playground."

"Playground?"

"Swings. Sand pit." Her voice was sharp and dire.

A third intake of breath.

"What now?"

"There are dead bodies everywhere. The playground is a graveyard. The old man is walking toward me. He's bringing the boy."

She stood as if welcoming these two strangers. Her eyes opened, but she was looking into another time and place.

"'Take him,' the old man says to me. 'Take him with you. Please take him before they kill us all.'"

She had a fourth intake of breath. Deeper, sharper than the others. A gasp that held the realization of her connection to the imam.

"His eyes. The boy's eyes."

"What about his eyes?"

"They're ice-blue."

Kurt slapped his hands.

The shock brought Dominique back to the room. Her eyes stared out but her thoughts were inward. Her heart punched at her chest.

"Breathe. Just breathe," Kurt said.

Dominique put a hand to her chest. She kept it there until both her breath and her heart calmed.

Kurt was steady and still.

"There are many guides that come to us the more we open ourselves to other realities. The more you see, the more your system will grind down your defenses."

"They weren't figments of imagination? The old man and the boy?"

"No. They're your guides, too."

Dominique's breath regained a regular rhythm, and her heart beat with a quieter pulse.

"And if I did save that boy with ice-blue eyes?"

"If he was the boy who became the imam you met, and you saved him, he might want to return the favor. If he remembers."

94

In the room where she'd met with the president, Dominique spoke with Bruton about what happened—that it was more than just the idea of a past life connection with the imam.

She told Bruton what the old man had said, of the young boy's ice-blue eyes, and if she had saved him in that lifetime—had saved the imam in that other life when he was the young boy—he might well remember that, too.

"How the hell are you even going to talk to him about this?

Dominique smiled.

"There's nothing funny about it."

"You asked me how I'll talk to him. So, let me answer you."

"Go ahead. Tell me. Tell me how."

"His brother."

"What the hell do you mean, 'his brother'?"

She told him the imam has a brother who's been institutionalized for decades in a hospital in Maryland.

"And how do you know this?"

"Mariam mentioned it when Nazir and I were with her."

"Sayyid Sarif's daughter?"

"Yes."

"And, how does the brother fit into all this?"

"I don't know. But I know he does."

"You're banking a lot on fate."

"That I'm still here is proof enough for me that fate is playing a part in all of our lives."

"That may be. But at some point fate stops and reality sets in. And when the imam finds out you went behind his back and talked with his brother I won't be able to protect you."

"I don't need your protection. I need you to get Hashim released into my custody. That was the plan. There's no room for anything else. I'm not going to let you sweep this under the carpet. You brought Adrien Kurt in to help find us when we were captured in Mosul. You let him bring in Catherine Book because your back was against the wall. You denied your experience in Vietnam until you didn't. You have to let this play out. Or, you can carpet bomb the world. Because that's where we're headed."

PART NINE

Into Buried Light

95

Monday, October 26

Dominique stood in the hallway outside Issa Malik's room in the hospital in Maryland. She could see the head of the psychiatric unit was intrigued why she was visiting the brother of the local imam. Vague in her response to his curiosity, she said she was doing research on the religions of the world and thought Issa could give her a unique perspective.

"So, you know about the hallucinations," the head of the psychiatric unit said.

Without missing a beat she answered, "Yes," even though it was news to her. She could see the response put the doctor at ease and he spoke about those within the Islamic faith who had suffered hallucinations.

Those imaginings, he said, were attributed to belief in the Djinn. He spoke of a study conducted to assess the impact of religions on the phenomenology of delusions and hallucinations.

"Fifty-three Pakistani Muslim patients with schizophrenia were interviewed in one study," he said. "The results indicated the more religious patients had greater themes of grandiose ability and identity, more likely to hear voices of paranormal agents and have visions of the same."

"That's not just the purview of Muslims," Dominique said. "And it doesn't mean they're crazy."

"I imagine your experience in the warehouse had a bit of the ontological as well, huh?" he said, prying.

"May I see Issa?" she said, cutting through the pompous bullshit.

"Of course, Miss Valen."

He escorted her into Issa's room.

Issa was a small man, compact in frame, nothing like the thin, angular features of his brother.

He looked up when they entered. His eyes were wide and daring when he saw Dominique.

She flashed to the story Julian had told her of Brian Halloway, the young soldier under his command. There was something about the look in Halloway's eyes, Julian had said, that would always haunt him. Dominique experienced a haunted look in Issa, as tears filled his eyes and a huge smile lit his face.

It was recognition, not madness.

Issa's tears and smile were a surprise to the doctor.

Dominique wondered if Issa saw the same tornado of sunlight swirling in slashes of gray dust and black smoke, like what Halloway had told Julian he saw on that roadside—like the smoke they'd all seen in the warehouse.

"May I have time alone with him?"

The doctor hesitated, but seeing Issa in a rare mood of happiness asked that she report to him whatever happened between them.

"Of course, doctor," she said, knowing she wouldn't.

The doctor nodded and left the room.

Issa gestured for her to sit next to him by the window. He may be a patient in a hospital, but whatever privilege he'd had in the outside world he claimed here as well.

"You're the journalist my brother spoke of." He had a voice like a young boy.

"You've talked to him," she said, surprised.

"It's not every day someone tries to understand us."

Dominique was unsure if Mariam telling her about Issa had been planned. Was she being played? Or was it providence like she'd assured Bruton?

"Did you know I'd come?"

"I'd hoped you would."

"Why?"

"Don't worry, you're not in danger. My brother cannot speak of such things. I can."

"What things?" she said, not sure where this was leading.

"The reason you're still alive is because my brother remembers you. But trust is harder earned than memory."

"He remembers me?"

"Yes. At the hospital, in the killing field, with the old man when he was a boy. I helped him remember. When he told me you'd come to see him, I told him who you were and had been to him."

Dominique's eyes narrowed. "If you're this prescient, why are you here?"

His eyes fired with delight. He bound up from the chair like an excited child. She could see he was full of things to say. And while she was aware this could go south—after all he was in an institution, and his brother an imam who secretly led a local terrorist cell—she knew her job was to be the vehicle for what he needed to say. And so, she listened.

"After your occurrence in the desert I knew what the evolution of it would bring. I didn't know the details, but I knew to tell my brother to be aware that there were others who would come to him, who also believed in a way out of jihad."

"Is this what Nazir sensed in his meeting with him?"

"Yes. My brother knew the air had filled with the scent of roses, too."

She could see he knew the amazing effect he was having on her.

"Did your brother have an experience like we did in the desert?"

"No. I did. That's why I'm in here. If they think I'm crazy, nothing I say will challenge their beliefs."

"You mean, ISIS."

"I mean all of them."

"So, you've been guiding your brother from inside this place?"

"You could say that. We're not all crazy here."

He was vulnerable in what he'd shared. And she could see his eyes now questioned the wisdom of revealing so much to her, so quickly.

He turned away.

Her hand rested on his shoulder.

He turned back, his eyes again laying bare the innocence of a child.

"You can trust me, Issa. We want the same thing."

96

"I trust the fact Issa Malik is in an institution hasn't escaped you, Miss Valen," the president said. Bruton was the one other person in this unfurnished room in a corner of the third floor of the Residence.

"No, sir, it hasn't. But I believed him when he told me the reason he's there is for his protection, or I wouldn't have asked to see you again."

The president closed his eyes and buried his face in his hands.

She could feel the load of decisions on him. The life and death choices he had to live with. These rooms held grief.

He looked at her with penetrating eyes, and she could see she'd added a complexity to the choice before him—a choice that took him deeper into a mystery. The mythic. Mythic in the way great literature is mythic. The way it transcends reality, yet exists in a form that grips the soul.

Homer. Aristotle. Shakespeare. Dante. Milton. Donne. They'd all tapped into that reality.

Not that she thought she was close to who they were, or what they'd accomplished, but she knew she had the potential to affect others like she'd been impacted. It was something of which she refused to let go. Bruton knew it. That's why he had listened to her. It is what brought them back to the White House.

"You're putting a lot of faith in the mystical," the president said.

"Yes, sir, we are. We have since this country was founded. We even print it on our currency."

He held her gaze. She wasn't sure if he was going to rebuke her or dismiss her. But she didn't flinch.

"You're certain of what Issa said about his brother?"

"That he wants the same thing as us?"

"Yes."

"I'm betting my life on it."

"Then, do the face to face with the imam and Hashim."

"You're sure, sir?" Bruton asked.

"There's no certainty in any of this, Charles. But if the imam is willing to go against his own mujahideen, it's in our interest to facilitate it. You are aware of the danger?"

"Yes, Mister President, I am."

"Good. We now have to decide what, if any, surveillance will be safe to arrange. Let the imam know the meeting will take place, and that you'll be discussing with him, and Hashim where best and safest to meet. He needs to feel in control of this."

"Yes, Mister President. He will."

She wanted also to say to him what she'd said to Bruton—that we will never reach the level of evolution the tablet speaks of until everyone reveals the scope of their operations, and the heart and soul of how they think. But she decided to not do anything that would jeopardize how far she'd come.

"Is there something else on your mind, Miss Valen?" the president asked.

Bruton gave her a look that communicated he knew what she was thinking. The look said, *don't fuck this up now.*

"No, sir. Not at this time."

"Keep me posted, Charles."

"Yes, sir."

The president left the room.

"It was wise you stopped yourself again," Bruton said.

"I know."

"Don't put that quid pro quo in the space anymore with him, or you'll find yourself in huge trouble."

"I'm not a fool, Charles. America's never been good at giving *this for that* at a level that could change the world. And, we'll never reach the level of evolution the tablet speaks of until everyone sees the evil they've committed, and gives up something they don't want to reveal."

She turned to leave. He reached out to her. She stopped.

"They'll use anything to justify what they do."

"And we don't?"

Are you certain about the imam?"

"Like I told the president, I'm betting my life on it."

"You're betting your life on a lot of things."

"If I didn't think it worth it, I would've chosen a safer line of work."

"We need to bring Catherine Book in on this, to keep an eye on all of what happens."

"I'll talk with her."

"I already have."

97

Tuesday, October 27

The young driver of the pickup truck flipped down the visor as morning sun shot across the windshield. His passenger did the same.

The truck fit in with the others on the road and drew no attention as it made its way through the streets of Fremont County, Colorado. It was the opposite of the armored entourage that brought Hashim here. The driver and the two men in the backseat were FBI. They wore work clothes and were armed. Hashim, in the passenger seat, was dressed like them, in a plaid shirt and wool cap over his head.

It was late morning when the truck pulled up to the white line passenger drop off at Denver International.

Two undercover agents who took over control of the situation greeted the FBI men and Hashim.

"Where the fuck you guys taking him?"

The agents ignored the question and moved with Hashim into the terminal.

The flight was full. In the exit row in coach Hashim settled into the middle seat, the two undercover agents flanked him. They secured their seat belts, as the announcement came over the speakers that this flight was headed to Dulles airport in Washington, D.C., and if that wasn't anyone's destination to please let one of the flight attendants know so that they may leave the plane.

Hashim smiled at the thought someone might be on the wrong flight.

But as the plane rose in the sky, Hashim's thoughts descended into the truth that had gripped him—he was the abhorrent darkness he had longed to destroy. He had refused to see the underbelly of those that had carved his hate—hate he had made his own. He had lived deep inside that world, and knew this would be his legacy. The paradox was that this darkness might be the door through which salvation came.

98

Wednesday, October 28

In the back room of a computer tech shop, in a mini-mall under construction, Dominique, Nazir, the imam, and Hashim sat around a rectangular Formica table.

Dominique had no idea where the meeting would take place until an hour before when Catherine remote viewed the unique storefront signage of the tech shop. Dominique also knew there would be undercover agents posing as construction workers in the empty storefront a few doors away.

If the imam was suspicious, so was Dominique, who said as much, revealing her fear this might be a trap. The transparency made the imam smile. He assured her she was not in danger, at least from him. He was risking his life as much as she.

The imam spoke of his brother and the sequence of events that led him to secure Issa's safety inside the hospital. He spoke of how terrorism rose from pain and loss, from a world falling apart, and how this had cultivated the belief for purification, and led him and many others to turn spiritual longing into violence intended to cleanse the world and create a transcendent state.

"We intoxicated them with love and spirituality for a dark purpose," Hashim said.

Nazir's jaw clenched.

Dominique knew this was a deeper level of experience for Nazir—for him having been indoctrinated by these men who'd preached hate, and now risked their lives for a chance at the opposite. She could feel the sting of his shame for having followed that dark path.

Of all the places she'd been in the world, of all the conflicts she'd reported on, all the violence and killing she'd witnessed, Dominique was more terrified in this place than she'd been halfway across the world in war zones. Terrified it would come to nothing.

In those foreign lands she'd faced certain death and survived. Here, she faced the possibility of shifting the tectonic plates of violence that had controlled the world ever since man realized he had a thirst for blood.

To get herself to understand them, she'd put herself in the mental state to join them. She needed to immerse herself in that danger, and knew she wouldn't survive in their world without it. She knew this daring, this baring was the reason she'd been trusted, why people were willing to tell her their secrets. It was in her bones, this availability to live in darkness. She'd sustained living in darkness, and at the same time trusted she'd recover when it was time to leave. But she didn't want to recover from this. They were at the center of a huge possibility.

In the beginning of her career she'd questioned the sanity of wanting to know evil, to be in it in order to know it. But every experience, every word she wrote, infused her with the insatiable need to know more.

She saw the three men looking at her.

"*Can we do this?*" she asked.

"There's a secret network being formed throughout the Middle East that believes as we do here," the imam answered.

He spoke of how Issa had once lived among the mujahideen. He'd believed what they'd believed. And he realized it was misguided. He was not the only one who saw this, and began to talk to those kindred spirits of another way.

"He had tapped into their souls," the imam said. "But for some, that was too terrifying, and they wanted to destroy him. So, to keep him safe, I said he'd gone insane."

"You've believed as your brother has for a long time?" Nazir asked.

"Yes. He opened me to many things. But I resisted. What happened to him wasn't so different than what happened to you in the warehouse."

"Religion is supposed to heal, instead it has made a world of enemies," Hashim said.

Dominique laid a piece of cuneiform on the table.

The imam picked up the stone.

Dominique watched, as his eyes seemed to read the text carved into it. He seemed to understand the words.

"Is this from the tablet?" the imam asked.

"No. The tablet is in the catacombs under the warehouse. These stones are the path to it."

"This one speaks of an elevation where souls will meet," the imam said.

"And I believe many will be gathered to that elevation," Hashim added. "But now, we must dig for the sorrow under the hate. Sorrow that has been masked by the tales of which we've been convinced—that power is all that matters. We've turned it into a virus, and haven't been able to sustain anything but the violence. What we have cultivated is meant to spread spiritual dread."

This has been our ideology," the imam said. "And it must be transformed in the deepest part of our collective soul."

"How have you been able to hold onto that when you've lived so long in the world of violence? When you've orchestrated so much of it?" Dominique asked.

"Not without our souls becoming darker," Hashim answered.

"There are others who hold these same two worlds inside," the imam said.

"How can we reach them?" Nazir asked, with a staggering depth of courage and curiosity that would help him lead an evolution.

"You have already begun, my son," the imam said.

99

Catherine's cottage didn't seem like much of a refuge to Dominique now. It was the middle of the night, and she'd shared with Julian her experience of the meeting. But he seemed deaf to what she had to say.

"What is wrong with you?"

"You're going to take away everything that lets them feel alive."

They were in the backyard, so as to not disturb the others in the house.

"You're not having doubts again, this deep into it, are you?"

"Not doubts."

"What then?"

"War sucks. But talk to most guys who come back alive, and they'll tell you life is boring stateside. And regardless of what the imam and Hashim said about holding two worlds inside, you talk to those who are promised virgins, and tell them it's a lie, and they'll put a bullet in your head."

"It's not all *Lord of the Flies*, Julian."

"Want to bet? The beast is only us. You want it to work. You want to see them underneath all that evil as capable of transformation…"

"We are."

"An imam with a crazy brother who's seen the light. Hashim manipulating you to get out of prison. A White House too easy to put you on the frontline."

"If this is still so hard for you, we're lost."

"We're walking through something we have no idea what it is. It's unseeable, unknowable, and uncontrollable. I'm terrified. And you're fooling yourself to think otherwise."

"I'm terrified, too. But the cost of not making this choice will continue to breed hate, bloodshed, and annihilation. It's been carved into us for centuries. It is not inherent in our design. We've been brought together, because in a time long before this, we made a pledge. Don't abandon that now."

"You've been pulled so far down this rabbit hole, I don't know who you are now."

"*Who are you, Julian? Who are you, now?*"

She could see her question was gutting him of the remnants of primordial armor he still wore.

Dominique remembered dreaming of the birth of a new world, in that hospital bed in Pittsburgh. What it would be like? Would it end the violence and hatred? Would she be part of a transformation? Or would humanity descend into a dark, cold night, alone, and forever? She'd lived in these pitch-black questions a long time. The desert changed that.

Every moment required a choice. She realized that as much as she'd pursued a life of truth on a razor's edge, the drug of comfort and doubt had always been breathing at her back, too, would always be there, desperate to not have another life elude its Stygian grasp. So, she understood Julian's dark night.

She breathed what she first breathed in the warehouse after the bomb hit. What she breathed in the catacombs when they made their way toward the light at the end of the tunnel, and stood before the translucent wall.

That language was in the pulse of this night. The same pulse that came from the tablet.

Dominique had been running away from something—from the truth of who she was. And now she found it—belonging to a tribe. She'd dreamed of living among nomads in deserts with abilities to heal. Now, she lived in the deeper truth of that.

It was a lifetime from sitting in her usual place, by the metal-shuttered windows, inside the never-closed American Bar in the Green Zone, Mosul, Iraq, waiting to make her next move.

What happened from here would take her to places beyond any she knew. She wanted Julian to be with her.

The air swelled with a vibration.

She surrendered to that trembling, and an invisible fire emanated from within her, through Julian, and into the night.

She reached for him.

He took her hand.

100

Thursday, October 29

Graced by the morning sun, the air swam with golden dust through Catherine's front hall.

Isabel, Jhana-Merise, Vincente, and Arama were there.

Dominique and Julian came down the stairs and saw them.

Dominique knew this part of their journey was done. She also knew she was part of a nervous system—with a heart and soul that experienced the same love—the same fear.

"Pneuma," Jhana-Merise said, as if reading Dominique's mind.

Vincente smiled. He'd stopped being surprised at the deep well of wisdom his daughter possessed.

Arama and Isabel were learning to be sisters again—theirs would be a longer journey to each other.

But all were at the center of this force now—at the core of *that which is breathed.*

101

Sunday, November 1

Nazir stood in the skintight kitchen of his Mosul home with its bullet holes and battered concrete walls.

A delicate silence passed between he and his grandmother.

The nutmeg colored headscarf she wore still softened the wrinkles on her skin toughened by the sun, the desert wind, and life.

She didn't seem surprised that her grandson had returned to her.

"I told you, you were spared for a reason, Nazir."

The air filled with that trembling sound.

"Yes, Grandmother. Blood for blood is not God's way. I know that now."

And as the late afternoon sun bathed the room in an Inca gold light, they embraced.

102

Hashim sat in his prison cell at ADX Florence, Colorado. His eyes closed in prayer.

He knew he would be here until he died.

Along with the isolation—his sentence—to not be part of the coming transformation, only its conduit.

His atonement would be to remember the violence he'd perpetrated. Those faces and deaths would haunt him forever. His one solace: the knowledge he was part of an evolution for which he and the world hungered. That thought gave him a fragment of peace within the cold, concrete life now his.

He prayed that what came in the next life for him would carry the purpose for which he'd become aware at the close of this one.

And in the darkness of his hell, he heard a sound. But there was no one with whom he could share it.

His sole companion was the chill that ran through him in this desolate place.

103

Monday, November 2

Frost covered the ground and beaded the trees and stone in crystalline winter. In the cemetery where her brother was buried, Dominique sat on the stone bench in front of his grave.

Her life hadn't flashed before her in the warehouse, when she'd stared at Hashim's serpent eyes, about to die—it did rush through her now as she let the weight of all that had happened fill her, in this place of the dead, with the dread of what might have been, and the choice made, to be part of the invisible fire that she and the others now carried in their lives.

Her brother had a parallel destiny—committed to freedom. But he was in his grave. She was alive. She knew she would see him again. And knew they would recognize each other.

They'd all been here before—brought together by a force they didn't understand, but now knew they were in its white-hot pitch.

This invisible fire waits, no matter the path. Past. Present. Future.

In every breath—in every echo of memory—a choice—the risk of remembering who we are. The ultimate cost, no one knows. The choice makes no promises. But it can no longer be avoided.

ACKNOWLEDGMENTS

I am grateful to Bob Gersh and The Gersh Agency. Bob has been my friend, agent and champion from the moment I landed in LA as an actor. His belief in me all these years has made all the difference. And when I told him I wanted to write he embraced it. Thank you, Bob, for your endless support.

Joe Veltre, my book agent at Gersh. Joe, your enthusiasm for the story I was telling, your guidance, and sending the manuscript out into the world made this possible. I'll never forget the week of Thanksgiving when you emailed me and said, "We have a publisher!"

Debby Englander, my editor at Post Hill Press. She read the manuscript Joe sent, and brought it to the publisher. Thank you, Debby, for your calm assurance and confidence in my work.

And many thanks to the Post Hill Press team: Anthony Ziccardi, publisher. Heather King, managing editor. You made the ride smooth. Devon Brown, publicist, who helped shepherd this work into the world. And, Rachel Hoge, production editor. Rachel, your insightful notes, and powerful response to my manuscript brought tears to my eyes.

Suzanne Williams at Shreve Williams Public Relations. Suzanne, your excitement with the idea of my story when we first talked, and the value you saw in it after reading it, thrilled me, and told me it was you I wanted to work with getting my novel into the hands of readers.

Jennie Nash, the creator of Author Accelerator, a company that helps writers bring their work to life. If you're a writer check them out. Jennie and her team are top notch.

Kelly Hartog. Michelle Hazan. Michael Raymond, coaches at Author Accelerator, each of whom contributed to making this book the best it could be.

Dawn Ius, a fantastic writer, and a friend. She's also a coach at Author Accelerator. She encouraged me to drill down to the next level of this story, introduced me to the exciting world of ThrillerFest, and is working with me on my next book.

Ava Homa, a critically acclaimed writer, journalist, and activist, who advised me in the world of Islam.

Hammad Iqbal, for his stunning photograph that graces the cover of my book.

Dr. Stephen Johnson, and the men of Thursday morning—for their friendship and authenticity.

David Dowd, whose support and coaching continue to point me toward a world of deep curiosity, in my work and life.

Herb Hamsher and Jonathan Stoller. They were at the beginning, and read the first draft of this story. Thank you, for the many years we shared and worked together.

And, my wife, Judith Light. Judith, your love, joy, humor, passion, generosity, and amazing talent lift me. This book is for, and because of, you.